RECKLESS MOTORCYCLE CLUB OPEY TEXAS

tied

RECKLESS MC OPEY TEXAS CHAPTER
WALL STREET JOURNAL & USA TODAY BESTSELLING AUTHOR

KB WINTERS

Copyright and Disclaimer

This book is a work of fiction. The names, characters, places and incidents are products of the writer's imagination and have been used fictitiously and are not to be construed as real. Any resemblance to persons, living or dead, actual events, locales or organizations is entirely coincidental.

Copyright © 2020 Book Boyfriends Publishing

All rights reserved. No part of this publication may be reproduced, stored in or introduced into a retrieval system, or transmitted, in any form, or by any means (electronic, mechanical, photocopying, recording, or otherwise) without the prior written permission of the copyright owner. The author acknowledges the trademarked status and trademark owners of various products referenced in this work of fiction, which have been used without permission. The publication/use of the trademarks is not authorized, associated with, or sponsored by the trademark owners.

Table of Contents

Copyright and Disclaimer ii

Chapter One 7

Chapter Two 21

Chapter Three 31

Chapter Four 43

Chapter Five 55

Chapter Six 67

Chapter Seven 73

Chapter Eight 81

Chapter Nine 95

Chapter Ten 107

Chapter Eleven 115

Chapter Twelve 129

Chapter Thirteen 141

Chapter Fourteen 155

Chapter Fifteen 163

Chapter Sixteen 173

Chapter Seventeen 181

Chapter Eighteen 193

Chapter Nineteen 211

Chapter Twenty 219

Chapter Twenty-One 227

Chapter Twenty-Two 239

Chapter Twenty-Three 247

Chapter Twenty-Four 257

Chapter Twenty-Five 265

Chapter Twenty-Six 275

Chapter Twenty-Seven 285

Chapter Twenty-Eight 299

Chapter Twenty-Nine 309

Chapter Thirty 321

Chapter Thirty-One 335

Chapter Thirty-Two 345

Chapter Thirty-Three 353

Chapter Thirty-Four 363

TIED

Reckless MC Opey Texas Chapter Book 5

By Wall Street Journal & USA Today Bestselling Author

KB Winters

Chapter One

Hennessy

I jammed on the brakes. This couldn't be the place. After driving day and night for the past two days to put hundreds of miles between me and trouble, I was looking at a nondescript barn that had a distinctly industrial air about it. Did I have the wrong address? Tell me he didn't live here. The red and black twisted metal sign didn't exactly scream home, but I hadn't come all this way to give up without trying. So I took a deep breath, sucking the fresh Texas air deep into my lungs until a feeling of calm washed over me.

When I reached semi-calm, I squared my shoulders and looked at the front door with all the determination I could muster. The GPS said this was Hardtail Ranch so it must be it.

"You lost, sugar?"

I turned at the sound of a honeyed southern voice, ready to wave off her concern, but the woman was...*beautiful*. Thick red hair fell in soft waves over bare shoulders that led to a killer body wrapped in a tight hot pink dress. Big tits, a small waist, and a smile that would have every dick in Texas hard for the next twelve hours, I wanted to hate her on sight. But there was a kindness in her eyes, and I needed that more than I needed to envy what the Good Lord gave her.

"I don't think so. I'm, uh, looking for someone."

She gave me a long, studious look and snort-laughed. "Aren't we all?" Another tinkling laugh fell from her red lips and she stuck out her hand.

"I'm Bea, but when I'm at the club I am *Be-at*," she said in an over the top French accent. "It sounds more exotic than Beatrice, don'tcha think?"

My lips twitched in amusement, but I nodded because it did sound exotic and beautiful. "*Be-at* is a very beautiful name. Fitting too."

She flashed a pleased grin and wrapped both of her arms around mine as she guided me to the door. "Come on in. I'll show you around, honey."

"Show me around?" What *club* was she talking about? "I don't know if this is where he lives," I said.

"If he belongs at the Hardtail Ranch, you'll find him here at the club. What's your name?"

I froze at the question, but there was no reason to. This woman didn't know me, and I doubt she knew the people I was running from, probably not even the man I was running to, so I shook off my concerns and gave her an easy answer. "I'm Hen."

Beat pulled back and looked at me in disbelief. "That name is far too cute for someone as gorgeous as you. Luckily the men will eat up the whole innocent virgin thing you've got going on." She pulled me through the first thick door before I could respond, stopping to bat her eyelashes at a baby-faced blond who wore a too-serious expression.

"She's my guest tonight, Ford. Hen, meet Ford."

I flashed a friendly smile, which he returned before his gaze slid back to the bank of screens that separated us. "Enjoy your evening ladies and stay safe."

"Always," she assured him and clasped our hands together before we entered another thick door. It must have been made from some heavy duty shit because as soon as it opened, a wall of heat and sound hit me, much louder than it appeared from the outside.

"Stay close to me, unless you see something you like, of course."

I did as Beat said, keeping my hand clasped in hers while she pulled me through a chaos of bodies. My senses were on overload between the loud, pounding bass of the music, the laughter, and the low hum of conversation all around me, not to mention the obvious sounds of sexual pleasure I found impossible to ignore. Finally, we stopped at a long wooden bar that looked like it belonged in one of the classy Wall Street hotels in New York or the fancy places frequented by Hollywood agents.

TIED

Not a sex club, which, it became move obvious by the second, was what this place was. A fucking sex club! Not that I was judging, I wasn't, but it was just my dumb luck that in escaping trouble I ended up in yet another place I didn't belong.

"I found a newbie," Beat told the woman behind the bar with the dark eyes and see-through black lace top. "This is Hen."

The woman flashed a friendly smile that wasn't at all lecherous. "I'm Hazel. If you need anything find me or ask for me." Her handshake was firm and capable and instantly put me at ease.

"Thanks, Hazel. I will." I hoped I wouldn't need anything but maybe, if this was the right spot, she knew Cruz. My gaze landed on the man now standing beside Hazel with the haunted green eyes. He was handsome but his features were too dark, too white to be the man I was searching for.

"What'll it be?" Her dark gaze bounced from Beat to me and back again.

"I'm celebrating closing on another million-dollar ranch, so pop a bottle for me, Hazel, would ya?"

With an amused smile she got to work fulfilling the order and I took advantage of being temporarily forgotten. I looked around the room in search of a familiar head of dirty blond hair. There were plenty of heads that matched that description but they were kissing necks, sucking on titties or being blown by men and women alike in various dark corners.

He wasn't here.

"Come on, let's finish the tour," Beat said, pushing a glass of champagne into one of my hands and grabbing the other. "This is the main room and plenty of action goes down in here, but back there is a smaller bar and a smaller room. In case you're feeling shy."

The smaller room wasn't smaller by much, and there was even more nudity and more sex. A threesome was happening in a cage hanging from the ceiling, the lovers seemingly oblivious to the audience watching them. "Are you shy, Beat?"

She laughed. "Not at all. I work hard to keep my body looking this good, and I love sex. All kinds of it, and I'm not afraid to ask for what I want." She pointed to a winding staircase. "Down here is where the real fun happens. Tons of different rooms catering to all kinks. You into girls, try the sleepover room. I like to start in there, get my pussy good and wet before the boys come calling."

Her smile was genuine and I envied her openness.

"You can try the romance room if you're looking to make love, the different BDSM rooms, harem room, rough sex...whatever you like.

While Beat spoke so casually of what was taking place in each room, I looked on in a kind of horrified awe. No, not horrified, but shocked. And intrigued. It had been way too long since I had a good hard fuck, the kind that made you come so hard you sprained a toe or threw your back out. Every room was a constant reminder of my distinct lack of orgasms recently, and worse, the reason behind that lack of orgasms.

"Wow," was all I could say.

"More than you were expecting?" Her melodious laughter sounded in the hall but it wasn't at my expense. "I felt the same when this place first opened up, but here's my one and only tip. If you see something that makes your clit throb or your nipples hard, give it a try."

"I'll, uhm, try to remember that."

I didn't want to reward Beat's kindness by telling her that I had no plans to get naked—or fucked—while I was here.

"No problem, honey." She laid an understanding hand on my shoulder and smiled. "If you need me, I'll be riding the face of some woman eager for a taste of some juicy cunt. Because this bad girl is hot right now! I hope you find the someone you're looking for." And with those words, Beat walked off towards the purple and red sleepover room, leaving me alone with my thoughts. And the impossible-to-ignore sounds of fucking.

"Thanks," I muttered unnecessarily because she was long gone by the time I found my voice. I wandered the length of the dimly lit hall, peeking inside for what I imagined Cruz would look like today. I hadn't seen him since the summer before my twelfth birthday. He didn't appear and that uneasy feeling returned.

I kept looking until I got to the end of the hall and wandered inside a large BDSM room, complete with leather, lace and velvet furnishings. A woman was strapped to some type of post while a man lashed her body with a leather flogger. She moaned her pleasure as each strap touched her skin. The man stood a few feet away with his cock jutting out towards her, long and thick and leaking. When I gasped, they both looked up.

"Sorry," I said.

"Don't be," she purred breathlessly. "Watch us if you like. We don't mind."

Even though I was intrigued by the look of satisfaction on her face and the way her nipples stuck out in pleasure, I shook my head and backed out of the room and right into a big, hard wall of a man.

"Shit," I said and backed away from the wall of heat. I was looking up into a pair of smiling brown eyes. "Sorry."

"No worries, sweetheart." He was good looking with long, brown hair, a thick beard, and laughing brown eyes. And maybe I'd be interested if my life wasn't turning into a Lifetime movie that had somehow ended with me alone in a sex club.

"What's the hurry?" he growled softly.

He looked friendly enough, but I wouldn't fall for that shit again so I took a step back.

"No hurry, but," I couldn't find my words and I tried to put more and more distance between us, but the universe hated me and put a foot of uneven carpet in my path just to fuck with me.

"Whoa, honey, settle down." He reached out and grabbed me around the waist to stop me from falling. I realized that too late and let out a terrified scream when his big hands wrapped around me and pulled me close to him.

TIED

"No! Stop! Get. Off. Me!" My words only made him hold me tighter, and I freaked out even more.

"A little help here," he grunted and bent over to stop my legs from landing on anything of value.

"Let me go!" I squeezed my eyes shut and kicked my legs even more frantically to save myself from this beast. Maybe they'd caught up to me already. Or maybe I ran from one piece of bad luck and straight into another. "Stop! No!"

"Calm down." This time the voice was softer and distinctly female, as were the hands that settled on my face. "Hey. Stop. Calm down." Her voice was firm and my eyes snapped open. "Hen."

"Hazel. What's going on?" She looked to the bearded man for answers, and I felt my body stiffen.

"Fuck if I know. I smiled, and she freaked out like I was trying to attack her when I was only trying to help." He was a big man but looking at him now, I could see he wasn't a threat.

"He's right. I'm sorry, it's just...hell I'm not comfortable here."

"It's all right," Hazel assured me. "This is Slayer. He works here. Sometimes. He looks scary as hell, and he's a big ol' flirt, otherwise he's harmless." She guided me to a locked room that looked to be some kind of employee lounge with two round tables, a fridge in one corner beside a counter filled with a coffee pot and toaster oven.

"It's obvious you don't belong in a place like this Hen, so what are you doing here?"

Wasn't that the defining statement of my life, that I didn't belong? My shoulders sank and I lifted them in a distracted shrug. "I came here looking for someone," I admitted and Slayer snorted and shook his head. "Someone I know," I clarified, sending a pissed off glare at his handsome beast. "I, uhm, haven't seen him in a while but I was told he lived...here, but I guess my GPS fucked up." Why I was annoyed or surprised was anyone's guess when this was pretty much how my life was going lately.

Straight into the shitter.

"Who are you looking for, Hen?"

"His name is Cruz."

Based on the way they both froze; it was clear they knew him, too. The look that passed between them said they weren't gonna tell me shit.

"Give us a minute," Hazel said and I nodded, watching them leave the room.

Outside their voices started in a whisper that was almost loud enough to make out the words, but they grew softer and softer until they disappeared altogether. Whatever was going on, they didn't want me to find Cruz, or maybe he didn't want to be found.

That thought sucked all the remaining energy from my body, and I knew it was time to go. I wasn't ready to give up, not yet. What I needed was a good night's sleep and a hot meal. Then I would try to find Cruz again.

I had to.

KB WINTERS

My life, and others, depended on it.

Chapter Two

Cruz

"Uncle Slayer is a dickhead, ain't he?" Looking down into the adorable face of Gunnar and Peaches' baby boy, Stone, always made me smile. The little fucker was cute as hell, if a little weird looking. He had his mama's light brown skin and coppery curls and his daddy's big blue eyes.

"I make it work, little man and I know you will too."

Stone looked up at me, my words finally stopping the flow of tears that I didn't think would ever end. Big wet eyes stared up at me like he understood my words, but I knew that was bullshit. The kid wasn't old enough for all that. At least I didn't think he was.

"I know you like to have Uncle Cruz babysit, but Slayer was supposed to relieve me of duty hours ago," I said to the little shit. The asshole hadn't shown up, probably still knee deep in last night's conquest. Not that I minded watching the kid. I didn't at all, but kids were a lot of damn work, and I needed my beauty rest.

Stone started to get fussy again, and I stood with the little bundle in my arms and walked the length of the kitchen, doing my best to stay out of Martha's way.

"Let the baby cry," Martha insisted. "Crying is good for the soul. Sometimes you just have to get it all out until you start to feel better. Isn't that right, little man?" The older woman stood close and cooed to Stone, distracting him from a big cry that had would have made every adult within hearing distance deaf. "You're fine, baby boy. Handsome, too."

His blue eyes stared at Martha the same way they'd looked at me earlier, like we were both an alien species he needed to figure out.

"He's cute as hell, but that doesn't tell us where the fuck Slayer is."

"Watch your mouth in front of the baby, Cruz," she admonished and smacked my arm.

"He's a man. He gets it. Don't ya little buddy?" Martha flashed me a look that said I was seconds away from cold coffee and no breakfast.

"Sorry," I offered and earned a smile for my efforts.

"You know what your problem is, Cruz?"

"I'm too young for you to take advantage of?" A wiggle of my brows, and she rolled her eyes.

"You're too handsome for your own good. No one has ever said no to you, and that's good for no man."

Martha flashed a look that said the conversation was over, pressed a kiss to Stone's forehead, and made her way back to the stove.

"No one is too good looking, little man. Remember that." I winked and held out my finger for him to wrap his little hand around, and yeah, I admit it. I melted like a bowl of warm butter. Kids were just too fucking cute. Especially babies. "Any of that coffee ready yet?"

Before Martha could answer, the back door flew open with way more force than was necessary. Ford appeared with a wide, boyish grin on his face. "Morning, Miss Martha."

She turned with a smile. "Good morning, Ford. How are you today?"

"Better, now that I smell your buttermilk biscuits in the oven, ma'am." I rolled my eyes at the way she blushed like a schoolgirl.

"Coffee is fresh if you're interested. Cruz needs a cup too if you don't mind."

"Not at all." Ford carried his big body across the kitchen, his heavy boots the only sound to cover up Martha's off-key humming.

"Thanks," I told him when he set the mug on the table in front of me. "Didn't you work last night?"

"Yeah, and I'm here to see you, actually."

I blinked at his words and looked at his expression carefully. As a prospect, Ford wasn't a patched Reckless Bastard, not yet, but he took his role as prospect seriously. "What's up? Do we need Gunnar for this?"

Ford shook his head and blew out a breath before he took a long ass sip of steaming coffee. "Nope, this is about you."

Now he had my attention. "What about me?"

"A woman came to the club last night. She was looking for you." The kid had more to say, so I nodded and waited him out.

"She stood outside the club for a few minutes looking kind of confused, but not like the normal shit we've been dealing with around here. She kept looking down and then up like she had an address that didn't quite match up."

There wasn't any reason for a woman other than my mama to be tracking me down, and I talked to her a few days ago. I always wrapped my dick before a fuck so I wasn't expecting any surprise baby visits either.

"What else?"

"She came inside with one of our regulars, *Beat*," he said with a roll of his eyes. Beat was gorgeous and freaky as hell, and she didn't discriminate. Not to mention, she had Ford and his baby face in her sights.

"Anyway, she freaked out on Slayer downstairs and told him and Hazel she was looking for you. When they left her alone, she booked it the fuck outta there."

"She leave a name?"

"Not that I got, but you can ask Hazel or Slayer." He shrugged. "Except for official membership info, everyone gives fake names anyway."

I nodded again because that much was true. I'd run into more Brandis and Candees at The Barn Door than I had at all the strip clubs I visited on leave from the Army.

"She give any clue what she might want with me?"

"No, but if you want, you can take a look at the security footage, see if her face rings any bells for ya."

Ford finished off his coffee and stood, smiling at Stone who was now fast asleep in my arms.

"If you need anything else, I'll be sleeping until it's time to go back to work."

I smiled, thinking of how much work the kid put into the Reckless Bastards and The Barn Door.

"Don't forget to take a little dick time for yourself. If you don't use it, you're gonna lose it. That's what I hear, anyway."

"Maybe you've been using it a bit too much," Martha grumbled from her spot in front of the stove. Ford laugh as he pushed his way out the back door.

"Very funny, Martha."

"I thought so. Get that baby in his crib before your loud voice wakes him up."

Another quick look down at Stone's sleeping face made me smile. Then it made my stomach clench. What if this mystery woman *was* trying to find me to tell me that a night, or even a weekend of pleasure, had resulted in me being a daddy?

"Shit." That idea didn't sit right with me. I wasn't ready to settle down and raise kids yet, especially not with all the shit that had been thrown at the MC lately.

"Language."

I rolled my eyes at Martha, mostly because her back was to me. and I didn't have to risk the wrath of her wooden spoon if she caught me. That, *and* I wanted to make sure she didn't *forget* to call me when breakfast was ready.

Stone began to fuss as soon as I laid him in the fancy bassinette thingy Peaches insisted we use. After all the Farnsworth shit, she couldn't stand for the little guy to be out of anyone's sight for any length of time.

"Don't worry Stoney boy, I gotcha."

When Peaches and Gunnar got back from their outing, I vowed to check out of baby duty for at least a month. The little guy was cute, but damn babies were hard work.

And that thought only made me think of the woman who showed up last night. Looking for me.

Stone wanted to be held, which meant I wouldn't make it to the club to look at surveillance footage anytime soon, so I kicked off my boots and laid on the sofa with his little body flush against my chest, so warm and tiny. He immediately calmed and the soothing sucking and cooing noises he made were the perfect soundtrack for my racing thoughts.

Eventually, I ran out of shit to think about, to stress about. With Farnsworth taken care of, for now anyway, life had gone back to normal, which is to say, it was pretty fucking good. The club was thriving and even the ranch had started turning a profit again. We all made more money at the ranch than we ever made working for the government.

Life was good.

Life was quiet. And drama-free.

Just how I liked it.

Chapter Three

Hennessy

I finally found Hardtail Ranch. At least according to the metal sign with two interlocking whips hanging from the wooden arch I just drove under.

After leaving The Barn Door, I'd gone over to the best-rated bed and breakfast in town, which wasn't saying much, and claimed my reservation.

Two fifty-something sisters with a penchant for gossip and a real hard on for the boys on Hardtail Ranch also ran The Opey Saloon & Lodging.

Thanks to Mary and Elizabeth Monroe, I found out a lot more information about Cruz and the rest of his friends. They lived on the ranch and apparently owned the sex club. It was a lot to take in before they gave me my key and showed me to my room, but I was grateful for the information.

Cruz's mom, Esme, hadn't said anything about him living on a ranch, owning a sex club, or, and this was the biggest piece of info of all, being in a motorcycle club. I figured she didn't know any of that, so when I called her this morning to confirm the ranch location, I kept it all to myself. I only told her that the journey had been long, and I hadn't found him yet.

Sitting in the rental car with the A/C blowing at full speed, I looked up at the giant white house, no the *mansion*, and wondered if this was the right thing to do. I didn't know Cruz anymore. The truth was, I'd never known him, not in any real way. His dad had married my mother when I was eight and Cruz was a much cooler fourteen. He'd never had time for a little kid like me, and before I knew it, he'd moved out, joined the Army and never looked back.

Yet here I was, ready to ask him for help. He was a stranger to me, and if he remembered me, who's to say he wouldn't kick me off the property and tell me to forget I ever knew him? But that was a risk I was willing to take. I had to take, not just because Esme had gone out on a limb to help me when I was a stranger to her as well, but because I had no other choice.

TIED

None.

Even standing at the metal sign, hanging at least a quarter mile from the front door, the house was massive. It was every princess's dream of a mansion, big and white and gleaming. Also, intimidating as hell. But the favor wasn't gonna ask itself, which meant I had to get my ass out of the car and go find Cruz. I took my time, practicing what I would say to him if he was around. If he was alone.

The faint scent of fresh paint still lingered in the air despite the oversized flowerpots on either side of the the wooden porch steps. It was perfect and homey, exactly like a Hallmark movie. That thought made me snort at the naivete of it all. This was a working ranch that housed a sex club for bikers. It was *not* a fucking Hallmark movie.

And that was good, because I needed a bit more badass biker boys than I needed a second chance with the boy next door. I knocked, twice, and waited. Impatiently.

After about a minute or two the door opened to reveal a young blonde woman with light brown eyes and a huge fucking chip on her shoulder.

"Yeah?"

"I'm looking for Cruz Anderson. Is he around?"

She snorted and gave me a long look that said she found me lacking in some way. If I gave a damn about this chick, I might have been offended.

"He might be. Who's asking?"

I rolled my eyes. "Is he around or not?" I didn't know who this chick was or if she had any claim on him, but I also didn't have time for petty bullshit.

"You sure you want to see Cruz?"

"Do you know some reason I shouldn't?"

This chick screamed troublemaker, so I wouldn't believe one word out of her mouth, but I would listen.

"Plenty, but that determined look in your eyes say it won't matter what I say." She shrugged. "It's your funeral. If you're lucky," she added so low that I barely heard it. But I *did* hear it. "Come on in, then."

"You live here too?"

She turned to, her brown eyes wide and sad and more than a little bit haunted, making me wonder what it was about this place that collected people in pain.

"Unfortunately. Don't worry though, I'm just the hired help."

I snorted at her implication. "Better than the last place I was hired to help out," I told her honestly.

"You're still alive, so I have to wonder. There he is," she said with even more attitude and pointed to a figure stretched across a green and brown checkered sofa. A baby asleep on his chest.

"Don't worry. The kid isn't his," she added before disappearing down a random hall.

Alone with his sleeping child, I took a moment to take in all the changes since I last set eyes on him. Gone was the lanky young man's body he'd had when he left, replaced by hard cords of muscles in his arms, shoulders, neck and legs.

His skin was darker now, maybe from the tours in the desert Esme had told me about with pride in her eyes. His hair was still a messy dirty blond color, though it was a tad lighter now, probably from hours spent in the hot Texas sun.

One thing that hadn't changed though? The sight of Cruz never failed to get my heart rate good and elevated, but the picture he made with the adorable curly-headed baby on his chest, pink lips twisted into a sweet pucker was enough to make my ovaries explode.

I didn't know how long I stood there, just staring at all the changes, but it was long enough that if the tables were turned, this shit would be considered downright creepy. I took one final look, checking out the short glimpse of a tattoo I spotted on his bicep and went to him. He looked so peaceful and the baby looked like an angel.

The little boy woke up first, gorgeous blue eyes staring up at me in wonder. I smiled down at him, noting the smattering of freckles across his nose that matched my own.

"Hello, sweetheart," I cooed. His mouth opened a little as he tried to lift his head, dropping it after just a few seconds as if the load was too much to bear. "You are beautiful," I told him, instantly feeling silly for talking to the little guy.

Footsteps sounded behind me, followed by a voice grumbling in my direction.

"For fuck's sake," said the girl who opened the door grunted and kicked the sofa. "Cruz. You have a visitor."

The second kick woke him with a start, and he sat up fast. Too fast, in fact, and I leapt forward to grab the little boy before he took a tumble to the hard wood floor.

"Whoa, I gotcha." With the little boy in my arms, I took a step back to give Cruz time to wake up and focus.

He gasped when he realized there was a baby-shaped void on his chest and looked up with a frown.

"Why do you have Stone?" His tone was angry and his expression dark, which worried me.

I held the kid, Stone, out to him while keeping a healthy distance between us.

"You sat up too fast and he nearly fell." It sounded stupid even to my own ears, and I realized how this must look to him.

"I wasn't trying to...take him or anything. It's me...Hennessy. Do you remember me?"

He took the baby boy from me and checked him over quickly, protectively. Another gesture that was unreasonably hot, particularly for someone who hadn't gotten laid in more than a year. That thought brought me to the reason for my visit.

"Hennessey?" he said, recognition dawning in his eyes. "Hell, yeah, I remember you. What are you doing here?"

Good to see you too. "Esme told me how to find you." It wasn't the best start, but I had to begin somewhere, and this version of Cruz was more intimidating that my teenage memories remembered.

"You talked to my mama?"

I nodded. "I needed to find you."

"Why?" His expression had gone from angry to blank, making him impossible to read. "Well?"

Cruz stood and became even more intimidating as he towered over me by at least seven inches. Up close like this he was still gorgeous as fuck with those blue eyes and that dark, honeyed skin, but it was a dangerous kind of beauty. A dark beauty borne of violence and tragedy.

"Uhm." I took a step back, hoping some distance from this intimidating man would help me regain the power of speech.

"Maybe this wasn't such a good idea." It was a stupid thing to say, really. Cruz was my best shot out of the trouble I'd found myself in through no fault of my own, but suddenly that didn't seem all that likely either.

"You came all this way. You might as well ask for whatever it is you need."

His tone was cold. Derisive. Like I'd done something to him. Like he knew me. Knew my life.

My shoulders fell in disappointment. "I shouldn't have come. Sorry to have bothered you, Cruz."

I turned away, unable to stare at him for even a second longer. Coming to Texas wasn't just a mistake, it was a stupid mistake. Why in the hell did I think Cruz would be willing to jump in to help a perfect stranger who only knew him because our parents were married? I'd wasted time on this trip when I should have been planning to disappear.

Permanently. The door swung open just as my hand reached for the knob and the dark-haired woman, Hazel, from the bar stepped in. Shock and recognition appeared at the same time.

"Hen. You found Cruz?"

"I did, and now I'm leaving. Thank you for your help last night."

I brushed past her and ran down the steps, headed back to my car as fast as my legs would carry me.

If I hurried, I might make it out of Texas before sunset.

KB WINTERS

Chapter Four

Cruz

Shit. I stood there for a second and watched her go. Her. Hennessy Oliver. My kid sister, kind of. I guessed. When I was fourteen, my old man married her mom, and we all moved in like one big happy fucking family. We weren't, and it wasn't anyone's fault but my dad's. He could have moved on with his life and his new wife and left me out of it. Sissy was a kind woman, probably the best stepmom a guy could have. And Hennessy? Well, she was only eight when I moved in, and I totally ignored her.

Or, I tried to, but those big green eyes looked at me like I was a hero, and I developed a soft spot for the little girl, which freaked me out. So I kept my distance. The last time I saw Hennessy, she'd been a knobby-kneed twelve-year-old with frizzy, red curls and green eyes that were too big for her face. I remember her toothy grin wobbled as she waved me off to basic training.

She wasn't knobby-kneed anymore. No, she wasn't a little girl either. This grown up version of Hennessy was way different than I expected, at least on the outside. She had the same pale skin and those same freckles over the bridge of her nose, and the same jade green eyes, but they weren't full of hero worship, and they weren't brimming with anything good.

The curves were new. Big fat tits and a tiny waist that gave way to grabbable hips and thick thighs that would fit perfectly on my shoulders.

Except she wasn't here to wet my dick. She was here because she needed something.

"Shit." I jumped off the sofa, and Stone's cry reminded me that Hennessy had handed him back to me.

"Sorry little man." I sat down and rubbed his back while I slid my feet back into my boots.

"Still killin' it with the ladies, I see." Hazel looked at me from the edge of the living room, one foot crossed over the other and a far too amused smirk on her face.

"A little help?" I held Stone out to her and with a soft smile, she took him from my arms and cuddled him, overwhelming him with her baby talk.

"Take it easy on her, Romeo. Slayer reached out to stop her from falling in the club last night. She freaked the fuck out. It wasn't a normal reaction, even though she didn't look comfortable inside at all. Something is up with her. My guess is someone hurt her. Maybe did something really bad."

"Shit." And I basically accused her of *wanting* something from me when it was clear, now, that she *needed* something. "I'll be back."

"We'll be here," she said, waving at me with one of Stone's little hands. "And protect the jewels, just in case!" Her laugh echoed behind me, but I was moving fast, out on the porch to see if she'd kicked up dust in her hurry to get the hell out of here. She was in the distance, marching angrily towards the street that led to Hardtail Ranch.

"Hennessy, wait up!" I flew down the stairs and picked up my speed when it was clear the stubborn woman wasn't gonna stop. "Hennessy!" Too bad for her that my legs were longer, and I was in much better shape.

"Dammit, just stop."

She still didn't stop. Her red hair flew angrily behind her as she marched forward, shaking her head.

"It's all right, Cruz," she said over her shoulder. "I really shouldn't have come here. I knew it would be a long shot or a bad idea, but I had to try. Don't worry about it."

I couldn't help but smile at the steel in her voice. Even as a kid she was a strong little thing, unafraid to take any criticism and just as willing to throw it right back. But this wasn't just your average Irish fire. No, this was some hard won lessons.

"Obviously, you need something, Hen."

"I can take care of myself."

"Maybe so, but just stop and tell me what the fuck you need. I might be able to help."

I sighed and waited to see if she would turn and talk to me. Was it only this morning that I was talking about how calm and relaxing life was?

"Hennessy, please."

She stopped and turned to me, arms folded so that a heap of creamy white tits pushed up over the plain white tank she wore, a pink bra strap showing. "Why?"

I sighed. "I don't remember you being this exhausting before."

She scoffed and shook her head, planting her fists firmly on her hips. "You never knew me well enough to know one way or the other, Cruz."

She was right. I hadn't really tried to get to know her. She was too girly, too nerdy, and too eager to please. I didn't know how to handle her back then.

"Okay, I'll give you that. Now tell me what's going on?"

While she decided whether or not to trust me, I took in the details I hadn't noticed, the ones that were so subtle that her curves overshadowed them. A freckle on her collarbone and on the dip of her top lip. The way her nipples pebbled as the breeze kicked up. That slight dimple that appeared at the top of her cheek when she nibbled on her bottom lip. The worry hidden behind layers in her green eyes. And the fear was unmistakable.

The longer she contemplated, the more I began to worry. What could Hennessy, this beautiful young woman, have gotten herself tangled up in? Of course, I knew women got themselves into all kinds of trouble, usually because of a man, but I wasn't getting that vibe.

"I haven't seen you in almost fifteen years. Whatever it is must be pretty important if you tracked me down."

Those words seemed to have gotten through to her because she let out a heaving sigh that contained the weight of the world on it. She looked past me, right over my shoulder, avoiding my gaze no matter where I stood.

"I guess that's fair. And true."

I soaked in the sight of her again. Hennessy Oliver had gone from gangly to curvy. She now had a slim waist and a big ass, and nice round titties, perfect to suck on.

They *would* be, anyway. If she didn't need help. If she wasn't in trouble.

I didn't fuck around with damsels in distress. Too much trouble.

"I did come here to ask for your help, but that was based on faulty information."

"Hazel ain't my woman."

She rolled her eyes. "I never said she was. I was talking about the baby. I can't and I won't...look Cruz, don't worry about me. Pretend this little blip never even happened and before you know it, I'll be a distant memory again."

Her words weren't bitter or angry, they were so fucking matter of fact, they pissed me off.

When she walked away, I reached out and grabbed her. She tried, giving it her damnedest to yank out of my grasp, but I was too strong.

"Talk to me."

"Let. Me. Go."

I released her with a smile. There was the fire I remembered. She and Sissy fought like crazy over every little thing. Hennessy wanted to grow up too fast, and her mom had been dead set against it. "Talk."

She nodded and folded her arms, but this time I kept my gaze on her face. I needed to see if she was being straight with me.

"You remember my dad, Homer?"

I nodded. "Hard to forget." I remembered that useless piece of shit. Even as a kid I knew how worthless that guy was. "What did he do now?"

Sissy left his sorry ass because he was a degenerate gambler. He gambled on any and every fucking thing you could bet on in this world, and usually he bet the wrong way. No, not *usually*.

Always.

"Right," she said with a grimace. "Well, he's in trouble. Again." Hennessy paused for so long, running a hand through her hair while she figured out how much of this story she wanted to share.

"Gambling trouble, I presume?"

She snorted. "I can't believe you remember." Her cheeks turned a bright red, and even though I was in serious mode, I couldn't help but wonder how pink her skin would be all over when she blushed.

"Anyway, it's been hard for him to get a game. He's been on a long losing streak if you let him tell the story, but the truth is he's got a knack for betting on the wrong horse, if you know what I'm sayin'."

I nodded, a smile touching my lips at her frank way of talking.

"How much does he owe?" Money was no problem. I could get my hands on enough to help—but not for Homer.

"Doesn't matter." Hennessy shook her head and let out long drawn out sigh. "The marker was me. It was me from the beginning, which means no amount of money will get *me* out of this."

She shook her head, angry as hell if those flared nostrils and the fire in her eyes were anything to go by.

"Who…fuck, who won you, Hennessy?"

My hands closed into fists, and I promised that no matter what came out of her mouth next, I would track that mother fuckin' Homer down and give him the ass whooping he desperately needed.

"You remember Buddy McArthur?"

I nodded. "The fucker who always bragged that his dad was mobbed up?"

"Turns out he was right. Only it's not his father Mickey who's in charge. It's Mickey's old man, Eugene McArthur, who's in charge of things. He's seventy-five *and* he's in the market for wife number four. Yours truly."

Holy fuck. "Homer sold you to a fucking mob boss?" It was...holy fucking shit. It was unthinkable.

"Yep. Not exactly father of the year, I know. That's why I ran." She was doing a damn good job of keeping a good attitude about it all, but I could see the signs of anger and tension around her lush lips and the way she kept her hands balled in fists.

"That and the fact that if I don't marry that old fucker in a week, he's gonna kill Homer."

"Shit." I sounded like a broken fucking record. But this shit was about as fucked up as the Farnsworth shit. Maybe worse.

Hennessy blinked, and I knew what was coming. I braced myself for it. Like most guys, I fell apart at the sight of a woman crying. She blinked furiously to hold the tears back and only a few brave ones slipped down her cheeks.

"I'm so mad at him, Cruz. So *fucking* mad, and he's an idiot and a stupid fuck, but I can't let him get killed." She swiped angrily at her tears and turned away, showing me her profile.

This was so fucked up. So fucking fucked up that I didn't know what to say or what to do. Hennessy's shoulders slumped forward and she let out a silent, gasping cry before shaking off her sadness and her anger. She gave her eyes one final swipe and flashed a shaky smile. She was strong. Too strong for her own damn good and I knew what I had to do.

"How can I help?"

Chapter Five

Hennessy

"You could marry me," I told him. It wasn't the most elegant proposal, and it definitely wasn't romantic, but this wasn't about elegance or romance. It was cold, hard reality.

Cruz looked shocked. Hell, he looked shook. Those sky blue eyes looked at me like I'd lost some of my marbles. Maybe I had. Desperation has a way of making even the smartest person a little bit dumb.

"Say that again?" His words fell out when he dropped his jaw.

I couldn't help the smile and wondered when the last time this guy was at a loss for words? Confusion was his main emotion, but he also had a healthy mix of disbelief and mistrust, both of which I understood.

"I said, you could marry me."

I held my hands up to stop whatever he'd been about to say, mostly because I was terrified he would kick me off the ranch, and I'd be back to where I was…ten minutes ago.

"Hear me out, Cruz. Please. Hear me out before you say no."

His pink tongue darted out and swiped across his bottom lip. It went from one side to the other before slicking over the top lip, leaving me temporarily mesmerized. Cruz brought himself up to his full height, just over six feet, and shoved his thick beefy hands into his pockets. He gave a short nod of agreement, and though my heart misinterpreted it and lifted in hope, the rest of me knew he was only agreeing to hear me out.

"Follow me," he said.

We walked in silence for a few minutes, back towards the ranch and past the big white mansion. "What do you call this thing anyway?"

He grinned at me, and I swear, my leg buckled for a moment at that sexy smile.

"I call it the Big House, but Gunnar says that sounds too much like prison, which of course means I keep calling it that. Holden calls it the main house, and everyone else flips between the two. Impressed?"

I nodded. "It's nice. Seems like a lot of house, but it's beautiful. Sounds like a lot of people live here."

"Well, here and on the ranch. In the bunkhouse. But yeah, we congregate there for meals and shit. I'll explain."

It was a house for a family, a happy family.

"It's big as shit, but it's come in handy lately."

His words were ominous, and I really wanted to know what they were about, but one thing at a time. If Cruz really was open to the idea, that had to be my priority.

"Gunnar and Peaches live there with Stone, who you met, and Gunnar's kid sister, Maisie. She's just a kid too. Martha is the cook and housekeeper along with one of her daughters. The rest of us live off-site."

That was a lot of information, and I nodded as I processed everything. "Off-site from the big house or the ranch?"

"The big house, mostly." We rounded a red brick structure that looked like an old schoolhouse, but through the uncovered windows I could see a few sets of bunk beds and twin beds.

"Wheeler is still bunking in here most nights, but he spends more and more time with his woman."

"She doesn't live here?"

"Nope. She works at the hospital."

At the back of the red brick building we came to a sturdy looking cedar bench. It was made up of just six, maybe seven pieces and it was beautiful.

"Wheeler built this with Slayer's help," he said as he sat on the bench and patted the seat beside him.

TIED

"Who planted the garden?" Flowers had just started to bloom on one side and vegetables on the other. The clear greenhouse was vibrant with the color of new plants. Relaxing.

"Wheeler." There was laughter and respect in his voice that I wanted to know more about.

"Did it for Annabelle. He fell hard for the Doc." The words lingered in the silence between us, and I looked at the tomatoes that were little more than small green orbs. For a second I wondered what it would be like to have someone plant tomatoes for me.

"So, how'd you end up here?"

He shrugged. "After the Army I didn't have a plan. Didn't really want one if I'm being honest. I went from being under my dad's roof to the drill sergeant's to sleeping in tents in hell. I found this place by accident, and I've been here ever since."

That was a nice story but there was a lot missing from it, but again, that was a conversation for another time.

"Are you seeing someone? Married already?"

His silence was deafening on the topic, and usually that was a man's way of trying to find a nice way to tell you to screw off.

"No." He huffed out a laugh and shook his head, his gaze focusing in on the tiny white rosebud that would bloom at any moment. "I'm single."

"No baby mama or ex-wife hoping to get back together with you?"

Cruz cocked a dirty blond brow at me, his blue eyes sparkling with humor. "None at all."

That was good, at least. It meant his hesitation had to do with something else.

"All right, Cruz. Tell me to go away or tell me what you're thinking."

He gave me another one of those looks that said he either wanted to strangle me or undress me. I did my best to control the shiver that ripped through me.

"I'm thinking that you must be out of your damn mind." He blew out a breath and raked both hands through his thick hair that was badly in need of a haircut. "Worse, I must be out of my mind for even considering it."

I understood that emotion all too well.

"Don't feel obligated to say yes, Cruz. You have a life here, and it wasn't right of me to come here and mess it all up."

"So why did you?"

Ouch. I shrugged. "I knew you were in the military, so I asked Esme how to get in touch with you. I saw some articles and photos of you on the internet, kicking ass, and taking names. I figured if you couldn't help me, then I'd fake my death and live off the grid until I'm dead."

"Not a very elaborate plan."

"I'm not a very elaborate girl. As soon as Homer told me what he'd done, I went home and packed a bag, emptied out my bank account, and hit the road. I was in Denver by the time I realized I needed a better plan than driving across the country. And without a plan, I'd run out of money real fast."

"Mama told you to find me?"

"To be fair, I asked if she knew how I could find you, and well, you know how your mom is. She's so kind and she gives such good hugs that I ended up telling her most of it and she insisted I find you." I blew out a breath, thinking of the way Esme had gathered me in her arms and told me it would all work out.

"If you say no, I'll just tell her that I changed my mind."

"Why would you do that?"

"Because this isn't your problem. I have to ask, but you don't have to say yes."

"Right, and have your death on my hands? I don't think so, sweetheart."

That wasn't a happy proclamation, but I guessed I shouldn't have expected anything else.

"If you say no, none of this is on you, Cruz."

I stood and turned to look down at him. "I figured if I was already married, then Eugene might let Homer work off the debt. But halfway here I realized how stupid that was."

I didn't want to say the next part, because I wasn't sure if it would offend him or not, so I took a deep breath and searched for the words.

"What changed your mind?"

"Honestly? Those twin old ladies at the B&B said you and your friends were bad asses. Good in a pinch. I figured the old fuckwad might be hesitant to make an enemy out of a motorcycle club."

His lips twitched. "That wasn't so hard to say, was it?"

"I didn't know what to call it, and I didn't want to piss you off in case there's a chance you're thinking about it."

"And if I wasn't?"

I shrugged. "Then pissing you off won't matter because you won't help, and I probably will never see you again."

His smile returned, and I wished I was still sitting because, holy hell, it was a potent thing, his smile.

"Makes sense. Too bad you're not thinking of one important thing."

"What's that?"

I'd thought of nothing but this proposal, and what I'd be willing to give up or do, to make it happen.

"We're strangers. We were kids when we knew each other, and, as you pointed out, we didn't know each other at all. Fifteen years have passed since then."

He was right. "Okay." It was a valid point, and I wouldn't beg him to help, even though I really fucking wanted to. "Thanks for listening, I guess."

He growled, and I took a step back, not out of fear, but because distance was key right now.

"You understand my hesitation, don't you? Some random chick shows up and asks me to marry her to protect her from a mob boss. How do I know you're not lying? How do I know you're not already married to this old man and looking for a young idiot to kill him so you can make off with his cash?"

There was a darkness, maybe it was anger, I didn't know, burning in his eyes, and I took another step back.

"Right. Okay. If you change your mind, I'll be at Opey Saloon & Lodging until morning when you're ready to talk."

He nodded, and I turned to leave. "I'm not sure I'll ever be ready, Hennessy."

Even though he couldn't see me, I nodded as I walked away. It was a big ask. I knew it, so his rejection wasn't all that surprising.

It hurt like hell and made my life more difficult, but it wasn't surprising. I barely knew the guy.

Chapter Six

Cruz

"Oh yeah. Lick that asshole!" A blonde woman was kneeling behind a ripped redheaded dude with his ass cheeks spread apart, her tongue deep in that dark crevice while he fucked one girl and ate the asshole of the one getting her pussy licked by the girl he was fucking. It was a strange, erotic centipede of fucking. I wasn't gonna lie, my gaze was riveted to that shit.

The dude was so *in* the fucking moment, unashamed to ask for what he wanted even though at least a dozen people watched, more than half of them men with their cocks out and in their hands. Stroking hungrily, at the women or the ginger. I didn't fucking know, and I didn't particularly care. We all had our kinks and without them, The Barn Door wouldn't exist.

"I'm. Gonna. Oh, God, I'm gonna....come!" The blonde who was getting her asshole and pussy licked at the same time shouted over and over, letting everyone on the whole fucking floor know that her orgasm was imminent. The dude slid his middle finger into her slick, rosy asshole, pumping in and out while she fucked the brunette's face hard and fast.

"Oh, fuck!" His roar tore through the air, causing a few gasps to go up over the room, as the blonde on her knees shoved her tongue deep in his asshole while she massaged his balls. His hips jerked as he came on a growl, pumping hard into the brunette until he was empty. Then the blonde collapsed on top of the brunette, with the dude on top of her.

"Fuck!" His body trembled and vibrated with pleasure, a smile crossed his face.

Aside from the heavy breathing on the bed, there was even more in the gallery as men and women, and a few couples, worked themselves into a frenzy just watching the sexy foursome. It was all in a day's work. When all three turned their attention to the blonde, who was still on her knees, each of them looking hungry and horny all over again, I walked away to check on the other rooms.

TIED

A perk of the job was that I got to watch all kinds of people get their freak on, fuck how they wanted to fuck. It was kind of a rush, watching people fuck who fucked like no one was watching. They went all in and they did it all in the name of pleasure. This place wasn't just work for me. It was the perfect way to get my dick wet with all kinds of freaks who didn't want anything more than a few fucks.

But dammit, my mind was back to Hennessy. Again. She'd been on my mind since she left the ranch two days ago. She was probably halfway to Timbuktu by now. I hadn't made up my mind about helping her, though, I guess by *not* reaching out, I had subconsciously made up my mind.

Hadn't I?

"There you are." Hazel's voice pulled me from my thoughts, and I looked up with a grin. "Done perving on the guests?"

I turned to the room in front of me where a woman was slowly sliding a strap-on cock the size of my forearm into a smallish dude with a ball gag in his mouth. The look in his eyes was pure ecstasy.

It wasn't my thing but I watched for a few seconds longer than I wanted, just to fuck with Hazel, then I turned back to her. "Now I am. What's up?"

"Ford has a message for you." She handed me a slip of paper, and I shoved it in my pocket. "What?"

"Just tell me what it says." I liked Hazel. Hell, I liked all the girlfriends and soon-to-be wives of the Reckless Bastards, but damn they were a nosy bunch.

"Fine," she rolled her eyes. "Hen hasn't left Opey yet. She just moved to a cheaper place to stay even though the twins offered to discount her room."

So much for avoiding making the decision for me. "And?"

"What the fuck do you mean, *and*?" she growled and pushed at my shoulder. "Go get her. Give her whatever help she needs. This is what you guys do."

"I liked you better when you were shy and quiet."

TIED

"Yeah? Well I liked you better when you were willing to help a person in need." She winked and stuck her tongue out, Hazel speak for *no hard feelings,* and sauntered off to boost our booze sales.

I wondered if Hazel would change her tune if she knew what kind of help Hennessy needed. Marriage. It was a big fucking commitment, one my old man hadn't been able to honor the first time around. It was meant to be a forever kind of thing, which is why I shied away from it. Well, that and spending more than a decade at war. It had never really been in my plans.

But this marriage would be for a good cause, helping a woman in need. Because if I did this, it would be for Hennessy, not her piece of shit father. Whether she knew it or not, Homer was as good as dead, and if she didn't marry Eugene, so was she.

And it wasn't like being married to her would be a hardship. I didn't know her, but that would change over time, and she was hot as fuck, so slipping inside her tight cunt might actually be a bonus. Just thinking about what I knew would be plump pussy lips had my cock growing hard, but my dick couldn't make this decision for me.

But my mind wouldn't let me think about Hennessy being tied to a fucking senior citizen and a mobster to boot. I couldn't let that be her fate. Oh, hell no! I *wouldn't*.

By the time I made my way upstairs to the back room, I thought I'd made a decision about Hennessy. A stacked redhead getting double-stuffed had my cock and my mind swinging the other way.

When a gunshot sounded in the main room, I took off at a full sprint, gun in my hand as I braced for action. All thoughts of sexy redheads and marriage proposals forgotten.

Chapter Seven

Hennessy

I took one final look out the window of the small suite at the old Victorian B&B, just to be sure Cruz wasn't sitting outside nervously waiting for a sign to come in. He wasn't out there, and I didn't actually think he would be. I gave him two days when I could only afford to give him twenty-four hours. He hadn't reached out to me at all, so I was calling it quits.

Stepping away from the window, I gave the room a final sweep to make sure I hadn't left behind any traces of my stay here. I made my way down the narrow wooden stairway to the large welcome desk where Mary sat, or maybe it was Elizabeth. The women were twins, but despite their advanced age, they did nothing to highlight their differences.

"Oh Hennessy, dear, you're not leaving are you?"

I nodded at the maternal way both women spoke, like they were everyone's moms.

"I am."

Her silver brows knitted in disappointment. "I hope the shooting at the club didn't scare you off, because you don't need to worry about it. Those boys have everything well in hand."

"Shooting? I didn't hear about a shooting."

I'd also spent most of the past two days in my room, planning. Plotting. Imagining what my new life would be like a few weeks from now.

"You haven't?" Her eyes lit with glee, and I knew this was Elizabeth. Mary loved to gossip, but she didn't have the same level of excitement as her sister.

"Well let me tell you," she said and settled back into her seat, hands folded on the desk in front of her.

The kitchen door swung open and Mary appeared, a frown on her face when she took in my bag on the floor beside me.

"You're leaving. Is it because of the shooting?"

"No," I assured her. "I was only here for a short visit."

"Oh good," Mary said and leaned against the desk on her forearm, the same gleam in her eyes.

"Such a sad story. One of the club members managed to get a gun inside because, get this, he was upset that his girlfriend was there with another man!"

Okay so maybe I couldn't tell the twins apart as well as I thought I could.

Elizabeth, I think, smacked her lips together.

"I heard she was his ex-girlfriend and used his membership to sneak her side piece inside."

Side piece? Did old people use that phrase?

"Sounds dangerous," I said, happy that hadn't gone down while I was there. Maybe it was a good thing Cruz hadn't bothered to give me an answer. It sounded like his life was too exciting for me anyway.

"Dangerous? People can be mean and reckless, that much is certain, but those boys, they're good men.

They seem a little rough around the edges, I know," she put a hand to her chest.

"But they sure are a handsome bunch. Why, if Elizabeth and I were a decade younger..." Mary began. She shook her head as a vibrant blush stained her cheeks.

"But they look after this whole town. When some hoodlums messed up Big Mac's place, those boys stepped in and took care of the problem."

Elizabeth nodded. "They just stepped in and handled it. They didn't offer up any details, and they never take advantage of the fact, either. Helped Edna Mae get all set up when they startled the poor dear half to death and she ended up in the hospital."

"They take care of us," Mary insisted.

"Then you ladies and this town are very lucky." I said.

I didn't bother speculating that some of that trouble probably wouldn't have ended up in town if it wasn't for those *nice boys* because the women wouldn't hear it anyway. And if they cleaned up their messes, they were better than most men. That thought led to thoughts of the other man I was trying really hard not to think about, so I pushed them down deeper and pulled out my phone.

"We are. When they first moved here, I wasn't so sure about a bunch of bikers," Elizabeth insisted and slid the pay machine my way, surprising me that the old girls were so high tech with their pay options.

"But then we found out they all served their country honorably, and we knew they were good men. We don't go to *the club* mind you, but it's discreet."

So they did know what went on over there. It was another odd fact about this quirky town that made me smile. "Maybe you should go over there. It takes all kinds, I hear."

Both women giggled. "You're joking."

"I'm not. If you're curious, what'll it hurt? The guys will make sure nothing happens you don't want, right?"

That was enough of a distraction that I could let my mind wander while Elizabeth re-entered the transaction, half distracted as Mary mused on what it must be like inside The Barn Door.

The phone buzzed in my hand and I looked down at the screen.

Can't wait to see you on your big day! Xoxo Dad

My big day? Of all the selfish, fucked up things he could have texted me. My big fucking day? The nerve of him, like I was eagerly waiting to marry my high school sweetheart or some guy that was my true love. Not some random fucking old gangster dude just because Dad doesn't know when to stop gambling. I was so furious, my body vibrated with anger.

The clap of loud thunder came so suddenly; I wasn't sure if it was my heartbeat or the thunder. Lightning quickly followed, and I didn't need to be a lifelong Texan to know that meant the storm was close. Then the sky opened up and proved my unspoken point.

TIED

"Dammit," I said. Just when I was ready, if reluctant, to move on to Plan B, the universe stepped in to screw me once again.

Mary smiled and bent to pick up my bag. "Looks like you're bunking with us for at least one more day. We'll even give you the bad weather discount." She winked and wrapped her free arm around my shoulder.

"Can you give me a small room with a view of the back? The tree is really magnificent at night." The backyard also opened up to a fairly unkempt piece of land that looked wooded. Easy to hide just in case Eugene's thugs were closer than I knew.

"Sure thing. We used to neck out under that tree in our younger days, if you can believe it. That George Walker was such a hottie in high school."

Elizabeth replied, "I told you to stay away from him! He was mine!"

"Oh, hell, girl, you wouldn't even put out until—"

"—Okay, ladies, where's this room?"

Both women fell into a fit of giggles that I could still hear even after I was in my new room with the door closed behind me. They were nice women who didn't deserve any kind of trouble, so I promised to stay in my room and out of trouble until the storm passed.

Chapter Eight

Cruz

"What the goddamn fuck?" Gunnar looked around the room at each and every one of us, his blue eyes cutting a hole right through us. Rightly so, I mean the shit hit the fan while we were in charge, but holy shit was the Prez pissed.

"Well? Anyone have any fucking answers or something other than fucking excuses?" Gunnar shook his head, raking a hand over the short crop of hair that had recently started growing in. If he rubbed it any more, he'd rub it right off.

"We don't pat down our members, Boss." I didn't mean the words to come out so harsh, but it was the truth. All eyes swung to me, probably wondering why the hell I was stupid enough to say anything that would draw a target on my back.

"And where *exactly* where you?" Gunnar was in the mood to fight. I got that and goddammit, so was I.

I shrugged and walked him through my night leading up to the shooting.

"Doing a circuit downstairs to make sure no one was in trouble. Came up and swept the back room first, like usual. I was just heading to the main room when the shots sounded."

It wasn't an excuse but it's what happened. End of story.

"That's not fuckin' good enough, Cruz!"

His voice was like a lion's roar in his living room that was somehow smaller with all of us in it.

He turned his attention around the room like a periscope on a submarine until he found his next target. "Wheeler, got anything to say?"

The VP shrugged, taking Gunnar's anger in his stride.

"What do you want me to say Gunnar? The guy was a full blown member. He had every right to come in here, and like Cruz said, we don't pat down our members."

TIED

Guests were always searched but never our members.

"Now we know," Holden began, his deep, smooth voice cutting through the rising chatter of the MC. "Couples should have their own memberships or some shit, I don't know. But I think Wheeler is right. The guy had every right to be here and so did she. It's a fucking sex club, for fucks sake. Should we do psych evals as part of the screening process now?"

Gunnar glared, proof that his silence didn't mean he was no longer pissed off. He was, and I would be too in his shoes. But this was one of those *shit happens* kind of situations.

"No, we shouldn't," he said. "Fuck we *couldn't* do that even if we wanted to, but we have to do something. We can't have people offing themselves in our fucking club. Death has a way of killing boners."

"Not to mention the reminder that no matter how good the pussy is; women always bring trouble." Slayer's bitter words belied his smile and everyone laughed at the sentiment.

"We need to do something to get people's minds off this shit. Some flashy kinky shit that no one will want to miss out on." The idea was coming to me, slowly, but it was coming all the same.

Saint snorted. "Of course, Cruz's solution is to throw a party."

I flipped him off. "They do this shit all the time in Hollywood and politics. Distract them with something shiny and kinky. A fuck fest or some shit. Think about it."

Some of the guys argued with me just for the sake of arguing, like Slayer. But Holden hated having anything to do with the club.

"We need to get back on track. Not do extra shit that will bring in more strangers."

Wheeler let out a loud laugh. "It's a sex club man. People come for all the *strange* they can find. When you want to fuck the same woman, you get into a relationship, not a sex club."

He stared at Holden, daring him to disagree.

"Yeah, well, maybe *that's* the damn problem."

"Or its your old man attitude," I tossed in, because it was guaranteed to piss him off. "No one is saying you have to get your ass up in a cage and show off, Mah-Dick, so settle down. Unless that's an option," I said, turning to Gunnar with hopeful eyes.

"Fuck off." Holden flipped me off and all of us, but Holden erupted in laughter.

"Maybe later," I told him, but I was determined to get this meeting back on track. I wanted to track down Hennessy to see if she was still in town, even though I kind of hoped she'd already left Opey. Found some other solution to her problem and relieved me of the burden. And if I let these assholes go on and on, we'd be here all night. "But for now," I said, "we should consider a big flashy distraction."

Gunnar nodded, slowly coming on board with the plan.

"Good idea, Cruz. You run point, but I want all fucking hands on deck. Even you, Holden. Make sure this fucking suicide mess is a distant memory. Shit for the old folks in town to gossip about and that's it."

His searing blue gaze landed on each of us, waiting for a verbal acknowledgement of his orders. Once Gunnar got it, the meeting was finally fucking over.

I stood and waited for the guys to filter out of the living room from my spot behind the sofa, grinding my jaw in my effort to keep my words to myself.

"Somethin' you want to say, Cruz?"

I shook my head. "Nope." When Gunnar was in the mood to be a stubborn son of a bitch, there was no reasoning with him. Wheeler could get through to him when he needed to, but that was it.

"Say it. Go on." He was daring me. Taunting me because he was still pissed. I could still hear the rest of the MC outside, and though I wanted nothing more than a fight, I didn't want any club bullshit right now.

But he wouldn't let it go. He said, "Just fuckin' say it, man."

TIED

So I let him have it. "You're being an asshole. *You* were the one who vetoed metal detectors, even the subtle ones those rich fucks would barely even notice. Now you're pissed that a fucking cowboy made it into the club with a gun! This is Texas, Gunnar. Every motherfucker in town has a piece. Even little ol' Edna Mae. This shit wasn't surprising, and it was nobody's fault but the idiot who killed himself."

The words rushed out of me until I was breathless and panting.

He held up a finger.

"One fucking day. That's all I wanted was one *fucking* day with my woman without any interruptions. I guess it's my bad for thinking y'all could handle it."

"It was fucking handled the only way it could be!"

Everyone had made it home safely. The cops arrived discreetly and it was all handled as quietly as it could in a town the size of a postage stamp.

"This is a small town so obviously word got out, but we handled it no differently than you would have—or could have."

"One fucking day," he growled and got in my face. I knew he was looking for a fight, but too bad for the Prez. I wasn't in a fucking mood to back down.

"Should have thought of that before you had a kid. Another kid." It was a low blow, but I didn't care. Now we had two kids to worry about keeping safe whenever someone's past crept up and put us all at risk. So far, the Reckless Bastards had to deal with a never-ending stream of shit, which I signed up for, but not for this babysitting bullshit.

"What did you say to me?" He stepped to me, and I bumped him with my chest and made my way outside, hoping the fresh air would cool one of us down.

"You heard me."

"Say it again."

"Don't need to, 'cause you heard me. You can be pissed off all you want, but don't give us shit for doing everything we can with the limits you put on us."

The first punch wasn't surprising because Gunnar telegraphed the hell out of his hits. But I let the jab land so I'd have a good damn reason for the fist that landed on him. I smiled and my knuckles scraped against his jaw.

He growled out, "Fuck," looking surprised.

We went back and forth, trading punches when I gave him a hard push, sending him down into the dirt. Gunnar got up and wore his twisted smile, and I knew we were doing this shit. He charged forward until his shoulder landed in my gut, and we both fell to the ground.

He hit me. I hit him back. It was a man's fight. A release of frustration. A split lip. A bruised rib. A jab. An uppercut. A backhand. A knuckle graze to the jaw. We were brutal with our fists, and it felt good. Really fucking good.

"Ready to give up?"

Gunnar grinned and spit out some blood. "Yeah, right."

He charged and got me good with a fist to my side, and I lifted my leg, smashing my shin against him. We both fell down on something too hard and too high to be the dirt. A horn sounded and we both jerked up lightning quick and stared into big, green wary eyes.

Hennessy.

"Feel better?" I asked Gunnar, hoping we were finished with the brawl.

Gunnar turned to me and nodded. "A little, yeah. You?"

"Same. We good?"

"As gravy, baby."

He smiled and we stood there, smiling at each other like two people who now understood each other better. He held out his hand, and I accepted it, wrapping my free arm around his shoulder. We hugged it out.

"Cool."

"Yours," he asked, nodding towards Hennessy's shocked face behind the steering wheel that looked too big for her petite frame.

"Something like that." I watched him climb the stairs and go back inside, letting the screen door smack behind him.

"Stop letting the door slam!" Peaches' words made me smile, and I took a deep breath before turning to Hennessy, who, it looked like, had decided to stop waiting.

"You here to see me?" I couldn't shake the concern that snaked around my gut at the fear and worry in her eyes. She was doing a damn good job of trying to hide it, but she still gave away a lot.

Hennessy nodded and raked a hand through her red hair. "I heard about the shooting, and since the roads are finally clear, I figured I'd stop and check on you before I headed out."

Sure she did. "Thought you'd be long gone by now."

Sometime in my tone must have rubbed her the wrong way because, at that moment, her demeanor changed. The vulnerability was gone, replaced by brick and ice.

"Me, too, but the damn storm blew through, and I had to wait for the roads to clear." Her expression was blank and uninterested. "Looks like you're fine."

"I'm good," I said and wiped my face on the back of my sleeve.

Hennessy nodded, and I wished I could read her, because right now she gave nothing away. Was she angry or hurt? Her gaze bounced around the empty space on either side of me and then she nodded and shifted gears.

TIED

"I'm glad to see you're not hurt. Take care of yourself." She backed up and swung into a half circle, giving a half wave as she drove away.

"Wait," I called out, but not really loud enough to get her attention, because I had no fucking clue what to say to her. She was asking too much. Her favor was too big. But she deserved an answer, dammit.

"Hennessy!"

It was too late. Her taillights disappeared where the dirt road met the actual road as she left Hardtail Ranch behind for good.

I couldn't let that happen. I turned and hauled ass toward my bike.

Chapter Nine

Hennessy

What in the hell was I even thinking, coming to Texas?

The question played in my mind at least a dozen times before I was off ranch property. I mean, seriously, did I really think Cruz would swoop in and help me? That he would come in and save the day? It was like I hadn't grown one fucking day since I was twelve years old. I was still looking at those blue eyes and seeing Captain America, or some other gorgeous Prince Charming when he was anything but.

"It's fine," I tried to assure myself as I made my way toward the interstate. Traffic was light enough to avoid clogged, congested lanes but thick enough the cops wouldn't notice any one driver specifically.

I cranked up my music and pressed down on the gas, focusing my eyes on the patch of road right in front of me as I put as much distance as possible between me and Eugene's goons. The man was a lowlife criminal with no regard for human life. He didn't want me, but felt I was what he was owed, and he wouldn't rest until he got what he wanted.

My rental ate up the road, and the GPS indicated I was on the right path. In eighteen hours, I would arrive in San Diego. That was the first step of my plan, and the only thing I was focused on beyond the cars on the road.

A thump sounded behind me, and I glanced back, hoping I hadn't been rear ended. Thankfully it wasn't an accident, but a masked biker whose fist had hit my trunk. My foot pressed harder on the gas to put some distance between me and the angry man who was probably one of the ham-fisted fuckers Eugene hired to find me.

My heart pounded in my chest. *Who is this fucker?*

I sped up as much as it was safe to, wondering how in the hell they managed to find me so fast. I had no known ties to Opey and immediately I thought of Esme.

"Shit!" Should I call Cruz and let him know his mother could be in danger? Maybe later, when I could think straight. When I wasn't being chased by some asshole on two wheels.

"Oh fuck." Another thought occurred to me. What if this had nothing at all to do with Eugene, but instead was wrapped up with Cruz's sex business, or that shooting at the club?

Didn't these underworld types all know each other anyway?

Another thump sounded, which said my mind was spending too much time thinking and not enough time paying attention to what the fuck was going on around me. This time the biker had caught up to me, and the thump came from the passenger side of the car. Even though a dark shield kept his features concealed from me, I could tell he was staring right at me. It sent a chill through me when he raised his hand and pointed at me. Oh my God! Was that a finger gun?

I didn't wait to find out. I punched the gas again, but it was useless. The biker kept up with me every step of the way. Two more smacks and I looked up again, glaring hard at him.

"What. The. Fuck?"

He flipped the visor open and even at highway speed, I knew those familiar blue eyes.

"Pull. Over." I couldn't hear him, but I saw the words.

"Cruz? What the fuck?"

He gestured for me to follow him, and I nodded, wondering if I should follow him. What if this was all some elaborate set up? *Fuck. What do I do?*

Instead of stopping at the first opportunity, I drove for six more miles until we came across a giant, fully lighted truck stop with a diner, rest stop and shopping center. The place was crowded, which was perfect. I found a spot near a camera and waited.

Cruz moved gracefully as he took off his helmet and jumped off the bike, brows dipped low in anger. And confusion.

"I've been chasing you for thirty damn miles, woman!" His blue eyes blazed and his damp hair clung to his skin. "Why didn't you stop?"

"How in the hell was I supposed to know it was you? In case you've forgotten, there's probably a bunch of thugs trying to find me. They might or might not be on bikes. I don't keep up on criminal driving preferences."

The words tumbled out of my mouth in shock over the chase and relief that it was over, and oddly turned on at the sight of him hot and sweaty.

"What do you want, Cruz?" He had days, almost a week to make up his mind and call me. He hadn't, so why was he chasing me down the interstate?

He opened his mouth to speak and froze. A stunned expression crossed his face, almost disbelief. I guessed that he'd chased me for thirty miles and had no idea why.

"Shit. I don't know." He flashed a self-deprecating smile that was all kinds of sexy, but I was not in a mood for distraction.

"I'd like to catch up. Let me buy you a meal?" He nodded towards the busy diner with windows that wrapped around the entire building, his smile so enticing it was impossible to turn him down.

"Forty-five minutes. That's all the time I've got to spare."

He nodded. "Good enough for me."

I followed him inside the diner with the green and white décor that peppered the booths and tables, the menus, and the uniforms of the waitresses.

"Where are you headed on such a tight schedule?" Cruz asked as he guided me to a booth that overlooked the parking lot. We slid into our seats, staring awkwardly at each other while I came up with an answer.

TIED

"West. It's probably best if I don't give out specifics." If there was a chance Eugene's men were tougher, I couldn't risk my plan getting out.

Cruz nodded. If he was upset I refused to share my plans with him, he didn't show it.

"Why me?"

"Because Esme said you were a bad ass. I figured I stood a good chance at surviving this mess if I had a bad ass on my side, too."

He snorted. "I doubt my mama said bad ass."

"She did." She spoke about him with such pride, I half believed he was part superhero, just like she did. "She said 'My son is a bad ass. He can help you'."

He blinked and nodded. "Why does this fucker want to marry you?"

"Because I'm what Homer put in the bet, and Eugene won the bet. He always collects his debts, he's a fucking mobster. I heard he'd taken a really old family heirloom from some dumb fuck that meant nothing to him, simply because he'd won it in the bet. Asshole."

"You really think marrying me will stop this?" His tone said he was softening, but I knew better than to get my hopes up.

"I figured he'd be forced to come up with something else if I'm already married." And it wasn't just that, not anymore. Now I was desperate to avoid the fate at any cost. "Look at this shit."

I handed Cruz my phone so he could understand why I was so damn determined.

His blue eyes fell down to the screen, brows shot up as he read the texts, letting out a long whistle.

"That motherfucker," he bit out angrily, which kind of made me warm and tingly that he was so upset on my behalf. "Sorry, I know he's your old man, but what a fucking waste."

"Preaching to the choir, Dude." I wasn't about to freak out on him for telling the truth about my old man. "So I'm not at all motivated to do shit to help him out. But," I let out a long breath because the truth was, I'd been kind of grateful Cruz hadn't called me back.

"But?" His tone was encouraging, but the way he waved his hand along said I was taking my sweet ass time.

"But I really don't want to bring this shit to a place with a newborn, or any kids really."

He smiled at me, and I was damn lucky to be sitting down, because the force of that thing was potent as hell. Should be registered as a lethal weapon and I knew he knew it.

"Baby girl, the Reckless Bastards specialize in trouble." He practically purred the words and leaned in close enough that I could see the threads of dark in his blue eyes. "Especially the special kind of trouble."

He wiggled his brows to make me laugh, which I did. To stop the tingling between my legs.

"Seriously though, we've been through plenty of shit the past couple years, so we're well versed in it, and all of us have been trained by the good ole' DoD. If I marry you, all of that protection comes with me."

I nodded and let his words sink in, unsure what he was getting at, honestly. The arrival of our waitress gave me enough time to get my thoughts and questions together. "DoD?"

"Department of Defense."

Duh. "That would be great, but are you sure? I know this is a lot to ask of anyone, especially a virtual stranger."

Cruz shook his head and let out a weary sigh. "If I was sure about any of this, I wouldn't have had to chase you down the highway to give you an answer."

That was fair enough, but still.

"You're not obligated to do this just because our parents are married, Cruz." I had to make sure he knew that. "They have no idea what's going on, and there's no reason they need to."

"I'm not sure," he grunted darkly. "But if I can help you, I will."

"Why?" It wasn't exactly the most grateful answer I could have given, but I had to know. Everything came with a price tag, and the markup was often steep where men were concerned.

He shrugged. "Because I can. Because it's what I do. And because you need my help."

"Thank you, Cruz. Really." But nothing was that easy in this life. Not ever. "How can I repay you?"

"You do what I say until you're out of danger." His gaze was fierce, and I nodded, thinking I might like to follow his orders when and wherever they were given.

"I'll do my best."

"No problem. *Honey.*" At my glare he laughed. "What? I'm testing out pet names to see what I like. Sugar tits."

I laughed. "You're ridiculous, but remember, nicknames are a two-way street. Not that we need to keep up any pretense. Once the marriage is legal, that should keep Eugene out of my hair, right?" If that was the case, Cruz could get on with his life without me.

"Right," he grunted, suddenly seeming angry about the whole damn thing. I didn't try to understand

Cruz but, I would stay out of his way and hope this plan worked.

Chapter Ten

Cruz

"Home sweet home," I said when she pulled up to my place.

I'd had forty-two miles to reconsider this move, and I changed my mind at least once for every mile of road my bike ate up. This was either the craziest fucking thing I'd ever done or it would secure that spot in heaven my mama was so sure I already earned. It was too late to change my mind now, with Hennessy standing on my porch waiting to come inside.

"Is that gonna be enough stuff?" I said as a tease.

Her gaze followed mine to the leather bag she pulled out of the back with one hand and the canvas bag with the other. Big green eyes sparkled in the moonlight, and she shrugged. "For now, it will be. I don't imagine I'll need a variety of clothes."

Because she wouldn't be wearing a lot of clothes or because she planned to hole up in my cabin for her stay on the ranch? I didn't ask the question yet because I wasn't sure I wanted to know. And I still needed to clear this shit with the MC.

It was a good thing Gunnar was probably still pissed off about the shooting at the club, because he was gonna flip his shit over this news.

"Welcome home," I told Hennessy and pushed the door open before smacking the light on in the front hall.

She stepped inside and flipped on the lights in each room as she took in every detail, what few there were. I was sure the first thing she noticed was the lack of personal touches. There were two photos in my living room, one of me and my mama, and one of me and my unit. Both of them sat right above my beloved big screen TV.

"Nice place. All yours?"

"Yep. Want it in the divorce?"

Her lips fell into a flat, disapproving line.

"No, it's just cool that it's all yours." She looked around again, nervous and fidgety. When Hennessy dropped her bags I noticed the intent in her eyes and took a step back. She grinned and closed the gap between us. "Thank you, Cruz. Seriously, thank you." Then she pressed her body up against mine and wrapped her arms around me in a full body hug. Even though she hadn't meant it to be seductive, my body felt big titties and feminine hips pressed up against me, and *he* wanted to fuck.

I let my hands settle low on her hips, barely resisting the urge to slide my thumb across the strip of exposed skin at her back. Her round hips filled my hands, and I heard the gentle hitch of her breath. The sound went straight to my cock. "I'm happy I could help."

"You're not just helping. You're saving my life."

She pressed a platonic kiss to my cheek, but her nipples were suddenly hard and pressed against my chest, and I squeezed her asscheeks harder than I should.

"You're welcome." I managed to grunt the words out and stepped back, putting some much-needed distance between me and temptation.

She smiled as if aware of the effect she was having on me. Holy fuck, that pouty-lipped smile that made it seem like she was thinking about taking my cock in her mouth was her sweet smile? Good Lord above, I'd hate to see her put on a sexy smile.

"Really?" Her surprise was, for some reason, even hotter.

"Really," I grunted out.

She laughed, actually fucking laughed at my distress.

"On an entirely unrelated note, where will I be sleeping?" She bit her lip nervously, almost like she thought I might think the two *were* related.

"In my room." Her auburn brows shot up in surprise and then came the fire, making those jade eyes into emeralds.

"You take my room, and I'll take the sofa. It's a convertible." It was barely big enough for me but it was comfortable. And close by. To help sell it, I bent and rubbed the back of the red and white sofa I bought because it was on sale and turned into a bed. "No problem. Really."

"I'm fine sleeping here, Cruz. Probably nicer than some of the beds I've slept in."

"I'm not fine with it, Hennessy." She took a step back at my tone, and I softened my voice. "I can't keep you safe if I'm upstairs sound asleep and they break in and shoot you right here."

Somehow her pale skin went even paler, and she nodded absently, staring at the sofa as if suddenly picturing her dead body lying there.

"Right. Sorry." She was on the verge of getting emotional and it was intriguing to watch her beat those emotions back down until her walls were firmly back in place. Suddenly I wanted to know everything about her life since I last saw her as a twelve-year-old.

"I'm trying to be grateful by not intruding into your life too much."

It was a tough admission for her to make, and I appreciated it.

"I said yes, so this isn't really an intrusion, and if it is, it's one I've welcomed."

If not with open arms, with protective ones.

"Still," she insisted with a shrug. "You should be able to sleep in your own bed."

"Look, Hennessy. I said yes, but this isn't gonna work if you plan to walk around like you owe me something for the foreseeable future."

"But—"

"I'm not done." It was almost funny how quickly she snapped her mouth shut. "We're doing this. You will be my wife, and I *will* protect you. Don't question me about your security or my sincerity, and we won't have a problem. Got it?"

She licked her lips and nodded. "Yep."

"Good. You hungry?"

"I could eat. In fact, let me take a quick shower, and I'll make us dinner."

My brows shot up. "You cook?"

"I'm not twelve anymore, Cruz."

My gaze swept over her body filled with soft, feminine curves. "Definitely not twelve. Thirty-six maybe."

Her lips twitched and her gaze narrowed, making me laugh. "Thirty-four, actually. D if you're that interested."

I wasn't, but now that I knew, I couldn't stop seeing my hands cupping those meaty tits, rubbing my thumb over big hard nipples.

"Good to know."

She sucked in a harsh breath, and her pupils dilated, mouth slightly open in a way that had my cock standing at attention.

"I'm...I'll be back to make dinner. After my shower."

I laughed at her retreating form, watching the sway of her ass, letting the movement hypnotize me for a moment. Hennessy felt the heat too, which meant it wouldn't take too much effort to seduce my new wife.

Chapter Eleven

Hennessy

Sandalwood and oranges.

I knew that enticing scent. Cruz had me leaning in way too far just to get another whiff of his signature cologne. His bed and his pillows all smelled like sandalwood and oranges. Like chopped wood and autumn. Like man and the outdoors. The fragrance belonged to the kind of man who'd take you hiking and then toss you down on the leaves and send you to heaven as the clouds rolled by. I shivered thinking about that particular scenario before I remembered, none of this was real.

It was the kind of scent that entered your brain through your nostrils and grabbed hold of your good senses until you were ready to do any and everything just to please him. That sounded like a fun ride. I admit it had me grinning like a fool and squeezing my knees together to stop the throbbing pulse between my thighs. But I didn't need that kind of lure in my life, especially from a man I've been crushing on since I was a kid.

Fake. This is all fake.

That was the mantra I whispered to myself all through dinner last night whenever Cruz sent one of those flirty little smiles my way. Or, if he spoke and I couldn't be sure if his words held sexual intent or if I was just a sex-starved pervert.

I didn't care what the answer was, all I cared about was that I'd made it through this mess unscathed. Cruz would be my fake husband in a fake marriage built wholly on convenience and security.

Just because he was a sexy motherfucker with those sinful blue eyes and that slightly tanned skin that took him from boy next door to exotic treat didn't mean I had to fall apart. It didn't mean I had to fall at all, unless of course I counted falling into bed, which seemed more likely with every moment we spent together.

I could sleep with him, share his bed and my body with him, without giving him any other part of me.

I think.

I sure as shit hoped so because last night proved to me that we'd be naked together before the ink dried on the marriage license. I could barely remember what we talked about over dinner, but I remember the pulsing heat, that throb of sexual tension that coiled between us, tighter and tighter as the night and the beer wore on.

That was last night. Today was a brand new day, and I needed to think about something other than my attraction to him. For example, what the hell would I do while I was here, and more importantly, how long would I have to stay here?

Those were all questions I was pretty sure Cruz and I hadn't discussed last night, which meant it would go on today's agenda.

After a quick stop to the bathroom to freshen my morning breath and wipe away all traces of seven straight hours of sleep, I made my way downstairs where most of the cabin was located. The top floor was just the bedroom with it's own bathroom. Downstairs had a dreamy spacious living room with high beam ceilings and a stone fireplace, a mid-size kitchen with top of the line appliances, and two small rooms in the back. One was an office, the other Cruz kept locked, which was fine by me because the first thing on my agenda was coffee.

With the hot, strong stuff brewing in the shiny black pot, I was suddenly in the mood for breakfast. Cooking dinner for Cruz last night reminded me how much I loved to cook for someone. I wasn't a gourmet foodie, but I enjoyed a good meal. For the past couple of years, though, and for plenty of reasons, mostly work and previous relationships, I'd given up on me and what I liked.

With that thought, I opened the fridge and found bacon, eggs, and butter, the key ingredients for the perfect breakfast. Cruz wasn't here right now, and he insisted I didn't have to pay him back. But wouldn't it be nice to eat homecooked meals after a long day of doing whatever it was that motorcycle clubs did? I didn't know what that was actually, but I figured food was always welcome, and it was even better when someone else cooked it.

The bacon was on a rack in the oven when I heard the front door of the cabin open. Cruz's heavy footsteps were audible even over the low hum of the podcast that played in the background and his presence was too obvious to ignore. He took up all the oxygen in the room and the space, and finally I looked up. "What?"

His brows were dipped in a low, confused V. "Where are your clothes?"

I rolled my eyes, suddenly feeling very much the way I did when I lived with his dad and my mother, like a teenager who could never do anything right.

"These are pajamas. It's what adult women wear to bed when they don't give a damn about pleasing a man."

"Who says I wasn't pleased?" His dark look transformed into a wide, toothy grin that was more goofball than sex symbol but still, sexy as fuck. His glaze slid over my body, or what he could see with the counter between us. The look in his eyes was like a heavy caress, thick and slow like honey or molasses dripping down my skin.

"I'm making breakfast and breakfast is eaten in pajamas."

"New rule?" He arched his brows playfully, laughing when I nodded.

"Damn straight."

"What smells so good?"

You, I wanted to say but didn't dare. "Breakfast. Hungry?"

His blue eyes darkened to navy at my words, and he licked his lips, forcing my nipples to harden and press against the soft fabric of my pajama top.

"A half-naked woman cooking me bacon? What have I done to deserve this royal treatment?"

TIED

Cruz dropped down in a chair at the end of the table and kicked his legs out in front of him, smiling as he crossed them at the ankle. "You gonna strip for me too?"

His tone was playful, but I wasn't naïve where men were concerned.

"You want me to?"

His nod came slow and seductive, like there was a sexy beat pounding in his head.

"Fuck yeah, I do Hennessy. But not because you feel like you owe me something. Because you don't. And I don't do pity fucks."

"Good, because neither do I," I snorted and rolled my eyes at his suggestion, like I *would* fuck him in gratitude. No thanks, I preferred to make bad decisions because I wanted to.

The moment was charged all of a sudden, and Cruz stood, slowly closing the gap between us with his lazy gait. Those blue eyes bore a hole into my soul, keeping me rooted to the spot where I stood in front of the stove, a few beaten eggs in the colorful fiesta ware mixing bowl gripped in one hand.

Cruz was in my space. No, he was *more than* in my space. He *became* my space. The smell of him, the heat of him, all combined together made my legs weak and my pulse race a marathon. What really surprised me, okay maybe it didn't, was that my panties were soaked under my cotton shorts and my clit throbbed.

"Good to know," he said. His coffee-scented breath fanned my face, and I exhaled deeply. One thick finger traced the line of my jaw from one ear to the next and my breath hitched just as Cruz took a step back and went to the coffee pot beside the stove.

"How do you take it?"

"Anyway you want to do it."

"I meant the coffee." He snort-laughed.

"Yeah, uhm, so did I." I chuckled along with him. He turned to fill two mugs, and I snapped out of the stupor he'd put me in and got busy with the scrambled eggs. They were simple but with some butter fried shallots and garlic it was part of my favorite breakfast in the world.

"Damn, that smells good, Hennessy. I love a woman who cooks."

His words caused my skin to heat with pride, but it wasn't just that. I felt my chest puff out a little at the awe in his tone.

"Then that's something I can do to make your life easier. Right? 'Cause I love a man that eats."

He nodded and handed me the coffee. "Speaking of, I figured we should do the ceremony as soon as we can. I'll see if Gunnar can perform it, since he was ordained to marry one of the guys in our parent MC. We can do it here on the ranch."

I blinked at the rapid fire change of topic from breakfast to marriage in the blink of an eye. No wonder my mom always told me to be careful who I shared my life with. Shit, Mom.

"I think it's best that we keep this from our parents. For now, anyway. Things haven't been that great—"

Cruz held up a hand to stop my explanation. "Agreed. But we should make a little effort with the ceremony, just in case people are watching. If McArthur thinks there's a chance its fake or can be annulled, he might not hesitate to act."

Shit, I didn't even think of that. A small sigh escaped as I thought of my pitiful savings being depleted and all because of a fake wedding.

"I have some money saved so it won't be a problem."

He scowled. "You're not paying for this."

I frowned at him, still moving the eggs around in the skillet.

"I absolutely am, Cruz. You're already providing security, at risk to you and all of your friends. That's too much to ask. The least I can do is pay for this fake wedding to happen."

"Yeah? Where's all this money you've got to waste on a wedding? Tucked in the door of that rental?" I shook my head, unsure what he was getting at. "Did you stick it under my mattress last night?"

"No. It's in the bank."

He smiled like he'd won some big prize.

"Exactly. If McArthur has his people watching you, that goes double for your bank activity. As soon as you withdraw it or use your credit card for a deposit, he'll be able to narrow down your location."

That wasn't what I wanted to hear.

"Shit. Fuck," I said as I turned back to the stove, shredded cheese balled in my hand. I released it and turned off the flame as an epic level tantrum took over me.

"Shit. Fuck. Goddammit. Motherfucker!" Thanks to dear old Dad I was trapped. "Fu-uuck!"

"Damn, girl. You okay?"

"No, but I will be." My shoulders fell as reality settled in over me. I had three hundred bucks in cash on me and that had to last until this shit show was over.

"I'll pay you back every cent for the wedding," I told him and poured the cheesy eggs onto a large platter.

Cruz patted his flat, hard stomach and grinned. "Keep the food coming, and we're good. I wouldn't say no to the barely there clothing either."

He winked and I dropped down in the closest chair before my wobbly legs gave me away. "This weekend is enough time to plan a quick wedding, right?"

"More than." I would agree to just about anything to get this part over and done with. "If this is happening, I say the sooner, the better."

Slowly the tension I'd been carrying in my body over the past month lessened. My shoulders felt a little less tight and my breathing came easier, more relaxed.

Then Cruz's ever present smile dimmed, and my heart constricted. "One last thing. I have to run all this by the MC first."

"First? I thought this was a done deal. Please, for the love of all that's fucking holy in the world, don't tell me I got my hopes up for nothing. I could be halfway to California by now, Cruz."

"I know, and it is a done deal, but I have to clear it with them first. Technically."

I didn't know what the hell that meant, and honestly I didn't care. Cruz was just another man yanking my chain because he could. Why would he say he could help if he couldn't? More importantly, I doubted his MC would come to the aid of some woman they didn't even know.

"This McArthur fucker will very likely bring trouble to our doorstep, so we all have to agree to take out the threat, Hennessy."

I heard what he wasn't saying. If the MC didn't agree, I was on my own. Suddenly the cheesy eggs and greasy bacon weren't all that appealing. But what could I say?

"Let me know when you have an answer for me."

A nice hot shower and some real clothes sounded perfect. The alone time wouldn't hurt either.

TIED

Chapter Twelve

Cruz

I wasn't even married yet and already I was in the damn dog house. All because I was doing the right thing. The MC had rules, and I didn't just promise to follow those rules, I took a fucking oath. That shit meant something to me, and if Hennessy and her cold shoulder couldn't understand that, well good goddamn riddance.

Rant over.

Because there was no fucking way in hell I'd leave Hennessy on her own against the mob. She wouldn't last five minutes and that was assuming McArthur wanted her as a legitimate wife. My guess was he had something darker in mind for the pretty redhead, which pissed me off just thinking about it.

Slayer walked into the Sin Room and took his spot at the table. "Whoa, man. Who pissed in your oatmeal?"

He dropped down in the chair and propped his big booted feet up on the table. "You smile so much we were starting to think you were special or something."

I flipped him off, but I knew Slayer wasn't so easily put off, especially when we were all still waiting for Gunnar to start this damn meeting. "I am special, asshole."

"Yeah, special snowflake," Wheeler added with a laugh. "Seriously though, you good?"

"Honestly, I'm not sure, but I don't wanna go over this shit more than once."

Wheeler nodded and turned his attention back to the door where Gunnar finally appeared, a big-ass grin on his face, and a big ass stain across his chest that none of us was stupid enough to mention. "What's up, fuckers?"

It looked like the Prez was in a better mood, which was good news for me all around.

"Ready to get started?" Gunnar asked.

He gazed around the room, his blue eyes missing nothing as he silently took in who was here, which was easy enough since every member of Reckless Bastards, Opey, TX, was present and accounted for.

"Just waiting on you," Wheeler said, his voice bland, almost bored.

Gunnar made his way to the head of the table, and I felt my throat close up. I don't know why the fuck I was so worried about approaching him about this, not when we'd gone to battle damn near every time a female showed up on Hardtail Ranch.

Peaches had brought her own trouble, right along with Hazel and Aspen and now Hennessy. The Doc was the only woman who gave more than she took.

"The metal detectors look great." It was as much of an admission that he was wrong as any of us would ever get. But it didn't fucking matter. As long as they were in place, we'd never have to worry about anyone but the MC being armed inside the club.

"You barely even notice them."

Holden laughed. "Exactly how rich folks like the help, seen but not heard. Or is that children?"

Saint whistled. "Given Stone's lungs, I'm inclined to say that saying is about kids."

He shuddered, and I'm sure it was at the memory of the kid's last crying jag on his watch.

Gunnar sent a glare around the table to show us he didn't appreciate us talking shit about his kid's lungs. Then his blue gaze landed on me.

"Cruz, any progress on the distraction?"

"Working on it," I told him honestly. My mind had been preoccupied lately, but I had a ton of notes on what I wanted to accomplish. "Can we talk new business now?"

Gunnar's brows shot up in surprise. "You bringing new business to the club?"

"Nope. A woman, and she's in trouble."

TIED

I sucked in a long breath, my gaze bouncing between each of my brothers so they would know this wasn't an easy ask for me.

"Her father is worthless, not even worthy of the title, and put her in the pot against a local mobster. He lost and she's running."

The room fell silent while I told them about Hennessy, her father and our plans to get married. After my long meandering explanation, it seemed like no one even dared to breathe.

"Holy shit," Slayer said slowly. "Cruz is gonna get married before me. What the fuck is this craziness?"

That sucked all the tension from the room and everyone began to laugh and joke.

Almost everyone. "You already agreed to marry her?" Gunnar asked.

"Yes. If nothing else, it means he can't marry her, no matter what the MC decides."

On the walk over, I'd already decided that I would marry her no matter what. The only question was would we live here on Hardtail Ranch or somewhere else where I could keep her safe.

"I know this means bringing more shit to our front door, but I couldn't say no."

"Childhood sweetheart?" Holden, the besotted fool that he was over his woman Aspen, asked with a grin.

"Nope. Her mom and my dad got married a long time ago. Still married last I heard."

"Dude, you're marrying your *sister*?" Slayer said, smiling a demented looking grin.

"She's not my fucking sister."

Hennessy was never family because I barely considered my own damn father family after the way he treated my mom. Hennessy was never more than an annoying kid as far as I was concerned. It wasn't like we were planning to have kids or anything. This was an arrangement, nothing more. "We're getting married this weekend. I hope you all show up."

Gunnar nodded at my unspoken declaration. This was happening, period.

"Do you trust her?"

That was the question, wasn't it?

"I can't say I know her well enough to trust her, but I don't not trust her." It was difficult to explain.

"Hennessy was a kid when our parents got married, and she was only twelve when I left for basic training. So, I really don't know her at all. Except she was a nice kid and tried to make me feel like I belonged when I didn't."

I didn't want to take any risks though.

Gunnar sat back. "I'll have Peaches run a check on her. Eugene McArthur, too."

We could use all the info we could get on this old fucker.

Gunnar stared at me for too long. "And if we find something?" I knew what Gunnar was thinking but it still pissed me off.

"I gave her my word I'd help her out, and I will."

I didn't bother to bring up the fact that I was on board every fucking time the MC needed me. But I wasn't a whiny ass little bitch, and I knew this world wasn't fair so I nodded.

"If you find something that makes you all want to back out, we'll leave the ranch until Hennessy is safe."

"Leave the ranch? No fucking way." Wheeler shook his head, glaring at Gunnar to say something.

But Gunnar just nodded, like that assurance was all he needed to hear. Like it was a *done fucking deal* that I agreed to leave the ranch and take a break from the MC to help out a friend.

How could he agree so easily when I fought, every fucking time, like it was my own fucking life on the line? Yeah, it pissed me off. A lot. But acting like an asshole right now would only make things worse.

"If that's what you feel is best."

"Sure. Whatever."

TIED

I shook my head and stood, ready to bolt as soon as the fucking meeting was adjourned. I was the first one out the door, but I could hear Holden's big-ass footsteps on my tail. The man was slow as molasses, with long deliberate strides that were impossible to keep up with if you weren't a giant.

"I don't need a babysitter."

"Good because I'm too old to babysit grown men. What's eatin' at ya?"

"Nothing."

Holden wouldn't understand because he was a rule follower above all else.

"Bullshit. Something pissed you off, but good, I want to know what."

His deep voice had a way of trying to lull you into peace before he pounced, but I was too damn smart for that.

"Well if Holden wants to know…" I started and shook the rest of the sentence off with an annoyed shrug.

"You pissed you're stuck with that party idea?"

"No."

"So you *are* pissed off about something."

"No, I'm not." I wasn't. I just wanted to get on my bike and eat up the road until I needed to come back to the club and work my shift tonight.

"I'm fine, Holden. Don't you have a woman waiting on you at home?"

He grinned. "So do you, it seems."

"Not for long. She's mad I brought her here when I didn't have club approval."

"She's scared, and you offered her a lifeline only to snatch it away. Understandable."

He stroked his stubble and stared at me.

"What?"

"Nothing. I think this will be good for you, Cruz."

I didn't know what the hell he meant by that, and I wasn't gonna ask. "The same way you helped Aspen even though you hated her guts, I have to help Hennessy. She was a sweet kid and her old man is a piece of shit. None of this is her fault."

He nodded. "And helping Aspen was more than good for me. Not just because she's mine now, but it forced me to address some issues I was happy to ignore."

"I'm happy for you, Holden. But this ain't that. This is strictly a business arrangement. A marriage of convenience."

"We'll see if you're still humming that tune after you're married. But that's not what's eating at you. Spill."

I wanted to vent about Gunnar, but I didn't.

"I'm just pissed that my shit is dependent on all kinds of things when everyone else gets help with no questions asked."

Now that I said it, I felt like a crybaby.

"Never mind. Look, I gotta get outta here."

"I'm here if you need to talk, Cruz."

"Yeah, thanks."

I appreciated his calm coolness and the way Holden didn't let a lot of shit shake his peace. I respected it and him, but right now I just needed to be on my own.

Alone with my thoughts.

Chapter Thirteen

Hennessy

"How long you plannin' on giving me the silent treatment?"

The sound of Cruz's voice startled me from my own whirling thoughts. That by itself was terrifying since I hadn't heard his motorcycle or four wheeler drive up.

I took a deep breath to summon up all the strength I could to look into those piercing blue eyes.

"I'm not giving you the silent treatment, Cruz. I just have some things on my mind." Like marrying a complete stranger who was sort of family, but also a biker-sex-club-owner-veteran, and the scary mobster who wanted to wife me up.

He nodded and raked a hand through his hair, blowing out a long contemplative breath.

"I know you do, but you've been walking around in silence for at least two days now. What gives?"

I arched a brow in his direction because, seriously?

"What gives is that you chased me down and convinced me to stay but *still*, two days later, you haven't said shit about what your damn gang has decided to do."

"Club," he said automatically. If things hadn't been so dire, it might have been funny, the way they were trained to correct those who called them a *gang*.

"I haven't said anything because I haven't heard anything. I told you, when I hear, you will."

"Oh, well that's just *great*. I'll just hold my breath and keep my bags packed then."

I knew I was being a bitch, but damn men and their bullshit promises. I had enough problems with Homer. The asshole.

"Look Cruz, I appreciate the thought, really I do. You're as good as Esme said. But I think it's best if I just get outta here. I'm wasting time and only letting them get closer to finding me."

"Fuck. That." The words came out on a dark growl that, frankly, did some crazy fiery things to my body.

"Those motherfuckers aren't going to do anything to you. I already told you, I'm going to marry you and keep you safe no matter what, Hen. All right?"

I nodded and folded my arms, waiting for the next round of false promises.

"The only question is will we be living here on the ranch or someplace else."

That was a little more comforting, but I shook my head, unwilling to accept any of it. One thing I'd learned in my twenty-six years was that when something sounded too good to be true, it usually was.

"What's the hold up? Why is it taking your club so long to decide if they want to help me or not?"

"I don't fucking know, okay!"

The roar startled a gasp out of me, and Cruz held his hands up, looking horrified at the prospect that I was afraid of him. I wasn't, but it was comforting to know it might bother him.

"I'm as pissed as you are about it, Hen. After all the shit...never mind. The point is you've got me, if nothing else. Got it?"

Damn! That took some of the steam out of my ass, didn't it?

"I don't want to cause any trouble with you and your *club*. I appreciate the offer, but I didn't come here to fuck up your life, not like this anyway."

It was stupid to assume they were some kind of fucking Robin Hood group, willing to help out anybody who needed it. The old ladies at the B&B and the people in town were different. They lived around here and keeping them safe was a matter of self-preservation, not heroism.

"You could've said that a few days ago," he bit out and the unusual snark teased a laugh out of me.

"Pretty sure I did, and then some crazy biker chased me down the highway."

Not that it mattered. It was seriously time to hit the road and drive until my eyes couldn't see straight.

"In a few hours it'll be like I was never even here."

I stood up from the sofa and stepped around his big frame that made the room seem so much smaller, and escaped upstairs to his bedroom to retrieve my already packed bags. Cruz was on the phone, *my* phone, when I came back downstairs.

"Who told you to answer my phone?"

With an amused smile on his face, Cruz held up a hand to quiet me, and I barely resisted the urge to snatch the phone from his hand.

"I always try to be a good boy, Miss Elizabeth."

He chuckled, eyes filled with mischief as he looked at me.

"Yeah, she sure is a looker. I'll be sure to pass along the message." He ended the call and tossed the phone my way.

"Well? What did she want?"

I couldn't think of a reason the B&B ladies would call me, unless my card had been rejected. "Cruz?"

"Some guy called looking for you, but he misspelled your name when Mary pretended she wasn't familiar with the drink."

His smile faded slowly, almost as if he was trying to give me time to let the words sink in.

But it was unnecessary. "Good thing I'm getting out of here, then, isn't it?"

"Wrong. It means you've been stupid and worse, reckless while running from them, Hen. Your credit cards? Really?"

He shook his head like *he* was disappointed in *me*.

"Well excuse the hell out of me for not knowing the rules of being on the run from a fucking mobster!"

"You've seen a damn TV show before, haven't you?"

"Yeah, I just finished a show about a chick with a cool-ass dragon? Know where I can find one? Better yet, can you get me a plane ticket to Never Never Land? I hear it's gorgeous this time of year."

"Dammit, Hennessy, this is part of the deal. I can't do anything about that."

I nodded, acknowledging that my presence in his life had caused major upheaval.

"It's a good thing that I can." I shoved the phone in my back pocket and closed the distance between us.

"It was good to see you, Cruz. You grew into almost the exact man I thought you would."

I kissed his cheek and wrapped my arms around him, hanging on a little bit longer than necessary. He felt good in my arms. "Take care."

"Hennessy, wait."

I shook my head and kept moving forward before I lost my nerve, my gaze locked on the front door. My escape. I opened the door and let out a shriek at the giant cowboy with black hair and blue eyes standing there with murder in his eyes. He was so damn tall, I had to step back to get a clear look at him, catalog his features as another thought occurred to me. I didn't know what the hell Eugene McArthur's men looked like so I slammed the door and locked it.

"Shit. Fuck." I turned to stare at Cruz who just looked amused, which pissed me off.

"See ya!" I headed out the back door, hoping I could get to my car before the giant got to me.

"Hennessy!" I heard Cruz call for me but since he didn't seem inclined to help, I had to do what I always did. Help myself.

I rounded the cabin and noticed the cowboy was still on the porch with one hand shoved into a pair of fitted light blue jeans. Good, while he was thinking about the best way to get inside, I made a run for it to my rental. I didn't stop to see if he noticed or if I was in his cross hairs, I just ran as fast as my legs would allow with my bags in one hand and keys in the other.

"Okay." Inside the safety of the car, I could only hear the pounding of my heart as my fingers fumbled with the keys, dropping them twice and failing, three times, to shove the key into the ignition. "God-fucking-dammit!" Would anything go right today?

A loud bang sounded behind me, and I screamed, daring a glance in the rearview mirror where I saw a sight that stunned me. Cruz and the cowboy stood behind my car, arms folded and dark expressions on their handsome faces. Were all gangsters so damn gorgeous?

"Get out of the car, Hennessy."

Fuck that. His words stilled my fingers enough to get the engine roaring to life. I smiled to myself at the small victory and glanced back. They were still standing there, which meant I had to decide, them or me. It was no question really, so I shifted into reverse and tapped the gas, shocking them both the hell out of my way. As soon as was clear of them, I took a breath and changed gears, giving the cowboy time to jump in beside me.

"Hello, Hennessy."

"No! Get out!" I slammed on the gas and drove in circles, hoping it would fling the big man out onto the dusty road and give me some time to put miles between us.

"Hennessy!"

He shouted at me with a familiarity I didn't like, and I slammed on the brakes which sent his face flying towards the dashboard.

"Fuck!" he said, turning a thunderous expression to me.

I shrunk back, sure a meaty fist was about to rain down on me. Instead he reached forward and yanked the keys from the ignition.

"Goddamn stubborn-ass woman."

With those grumbled words, he stepped from the car, a hand to his nose.

"You'll have your hands full with that one, man. Good luck."

Cruz laughed and shook his head as he came to a stop beside the driver's door.

"Hennessy, this is one of my brothers, Holden. In fact, I'm pretty sure he's already agreed to be the best man."

Shit. "Oh my God, I'm so sorry. I thought…"

The man, Holden, held his free hand up. "It's obvious what you thought, and I understand."

"Still, I'm sorry about your nose."

Cruz let out another chuckle. "Apologize to Aspen. She's gotta look at his ugly mug every day."

"So do you," he grunted. "If you're in a listening mood, I came to tell you that everything checked out, and Gunnar says you're good. Both of you."

While those words gave me a huge sense of relief, they only seemed to anger Cruz. I couldn't understand why.

"Yeah, great," he snarled. "Thanks."

Even Holden seemed confused. His brows dipped into a deep vee. "No problem. We'll talk later."

Cruz nodded and watched Holden walk over to a golden horse, hop on like he'd been doing it his whole life, and rode away. Then, he turned to me, laughter shining in his eyes.

"I guess we've got a wedding to plan."

I nodded and stepped from the car since the keys were…not in my possession. "He took my keys."

"Good. I don't want you running from me again, Hennessy."

His gaze was gravely serious, his expression not giving an inch.

"I wasn't running from you. I was running away from that thuggy cowboy."

His lips twitched. "Can't wait to tell him you said that." He flung an arm over my shoulder. "Come on, wifey. We've got a lot to discuss before the weekend and

I have a shift at the club tonight, which means you do too."

He grinned at my dismay, and I knew then, someone had told him about my visit to The Barn Door.

TIED

Chapter Fourteen

Cruz

"Looks like your brother is having the time of his life."

The words tumbled out of my mouth on a grin, but Wheeler's displeased grunt turned it into full blown laughter.

"This is what you called me down here for?" He folded his big-ass arms across his chest, and a pissed off expression darkened his face.

"I ought to kick your ass, but I don't want you to have a black eye on your wedding day." His lips twitched, and I wanted to punch him.

"I'd still be prettier than you so have at it."

It was foolish to push Wheeler, but it was so damn fun I couldn't help myself.

"Besides, who wouldn't want to see all this?"

I motioned to the two-way mirror we stood behind, watching Mitch take on three women.

"That's your brother taking on three chicks, one in every shade."

Wheeler shook his head. "You're sick in the head, you know that?"

I shrugged and kept my gaze on the action inside one of the fuck rooms. "Look at that. That girl has her tongue so deep in his ass she can probably taste what he had for dinner."

Wheeler's lips twitched, and he shook his head, but he didn't look away. "I've got eyes, Cruz."

"Yeah, but you're not appreciating this. Now look at that other chick under him, grabbing his ass while he's fucking her face, begging him to give her more cock." I let out a low whistle. "That's the definition of cock hungry, man."

We should all be so lucky.

"And then, just because he's a fucking man, he's licking that hot long-haired chick like she was the last drop of food at his favorite buffet."

It was hot as fuck, even though I never wanted to see Mitch, or anyone else I knew, butt naked and getting their asshole licked.

"If you're so interested, go join them. Unless you're saving yourself for your wedding night."

Wheeler laughed at my look of dismay and clapped me on the back before walking away.

"I'll be in the office."

"Beating off to what you just saw?" I laughed at the middle finger he sent me before he turned the corner and disappeared into the rooms reserved just for employees.

Long after Wheeler was gone and long after I moved on from Mitch getting his freak on with the hot chicks, Wheeler's words rang in my ear. *Saving yourself for your wedding night.*

Sure, I'd thought about fucking Hennessy, almost since the moment she arrived, but I hadn't thought about it in practical terms. Hennessy and I would be living together, which was intimate all on its own, but her penchant for running around in next to nothing would be hard. Really fucking hard if she planned to live like a nun during our marriage.

But I remembered the way her eyes had darkened with desire in the kitchen. Her scent had wafted over the counter, mixing with the smells of breakfast. Hennessy wanted me, too, which meant I'd be getting my dick inside her in just a few days. That thought brought a smile to my face, and I continued down the hall, stopping to watch the mayor of Opey and his wife inside the harem room with a young blonde-headed couple.

Everything was going as it should downstairs, which meant lots of satisfied couples, tons of moaning, and lots of fucking lube. That meant all was right with the world, and I could make my way up to the top level to make sure it all stayed that way. If we had another incident here before I put on our big party, the shit would hit the fan.

"There you are." Gunnar's voice broke through my thoughts at the end of the hall. "I heard you asked Holden to be your Best Man. It surprised me."

It should have since we'd grown fairly close over the past couple years, but right now he wasn't being much of a fucking friend.

"Why? You don't even want Hennessy or her trouble here, so why do you even care?"

Just because we were brothers, family, didn't mean we got along all the time. It was impossible given the lives all of us led before coming to Hardtail Ranch.

Gunnar let out a sigh and looked me right in the eyes. "It's not that I don't want her here. I have a kid man, a little boy who means the world to me. That might be coloring my judgment."

Yeah, I understood that, but it didn't fucking matter.

"Fuck that, Gunnar. This is what we do, all of us. We've been trained by the best to run toward danger, to put our lives on the line to save those who matter to us, and we've done it at least twice for Peaches. Aspen. Hazel."

The more I talked about it, the more it pissed me off, but it was over and done with. No point bringing up the past.

"You wanna do something? You can perform the ceremony so we can keep it all in the *family*."

A smile lit up his usually scowling face. "I can do that."

"Great," I said sarcastically and walked away. The refuge of the staircase was just a few feet away, but Gunnar called out to me before I was far enough away to pretend I didn't hear him. "Cruz!"

"Yeah?"

"It's not personal."

I barked out a bitter laugh and shook my head.

TIED

"Right. It feels pretty fuckin' personal to me, Prez." Then I made my way up the stairs, taking them two at a time just to end this fucking conversation before I said something I might regret later.

I shoved away all thoughts of Gunnar and quickly scanned the back room so I could make my way to the front and keep an eye on my fiancée. And wasn't that just a fucking trip to think about, that I had a fucking fiancée, and it was Hennessy Oliver.

And Sweet Jesus, she was all grown up now.

Chapter Fifteen

Hennessy

Tomorrow I'd be married woman. A woman with a husband, an incredibly good-looking husband who wasn't really mine, but that didn't seem to make a damn bit of difference to my mind. Or my body.

The only thing I could think about was Cruz and that dark look he sent my way from across the club last night. It hit me right between the legs, making my clit throb and ache for the rest of the night. All the scantily clad men and women, bumping and grinding all over each other didn't help my situation. At all.

Riding home on the back of his four wheeler with my arms wrapped tight around what I now knew were washboard abs hadn't helped at all. As soon as we were inside the cabin, I made my escape upstairs and relieved myself in the hot steamy shower while thoughts of Cruz, naked and hot as fuck, played behind my lids.

Thoughts like that didn't bode very well for my life starting tomorrow, when Cruz and I would officially become husband and wife. He'd gotten up early to pick up the marriage license, which gave me plenty of time alone, to steel myself against my reaction to Cruz whenever he was close. Too close.

When tomorrow rolled around, and Gunnar announced us husband and wife, I couldn't let attraction get in the way of the favor he was doing for me. The really huge, gigantic favor that could never, in a million years, be repaid. So I shoved it all down as I shredded potatoes, pretended those eyes were the color of mud while I browned the ground beef and tossed a diced onion in with them, telling myself he was plain-looking. Average. And who in the hell had washboard abs over the age of thirty outside of Hollywood? No one. It meant Cruz was vain. He was a vain man with plain features and flat dull eyes. Oh, and he was in a motorcycle gang.

Why would I want a man like that?

Despite my efforts, by the time I could smell the cheesy breakfast casserole wafting in the air, my body hummed with desire. Arousal. And it was all centered on my husband-to-be.

Damn his good-looking self.

The doorbell rang and it was followed by a series of frantic knocks that immediately put me on edge. Had Eugene's men somehow found me? Had they been watching and waiting for the perfect moment, when Cruz was gone, to come and kidnap me?

"Shit," I whispered and scanned the kitchen for the knife block, happy to see Cruz kept the big knives there, too. And they were sharp. Armed with the long chef's knife, I made my way to the door and then stopped.

What the hell was I doing, answering the door when there were violent mobsters on the other side? The bell and the pounding stopped for a second and started up again.

"We know you're in there girl, so open up!"

I paused, troubled. The voice belonged to a woman, but not any woman I knew, and I realized as I took two steps towards the door, that I was being sexist to my own detriment. It was entirely possible Eugene sent a woman to disarm me and grab me while my guard was down. A quick peek out one of the front windows showed it wasn't just one or two women. It was a whole damn group.

"Yo, Hen, open up!"

That voice I recognized because I spent all night listening to Hazel laugh and flirt with customers while she slung cocktails. Feeling some relief, I went to the door and opened it up.

"What's up...ladies?"

Hazel stood in front, beside a tall curvaceous, freckle-faced woman with a wild head of copper curls. Both sets of eyes slid down to my hand, and Hazel grinned.

"Expecting company?"

"Never can be too careful."

TIED

I didn't know how much Cruz told his club or how much they shared with their women, but I didn't want to go through the tale again.

"Did y'all need something? Cruz isn't here."

"We know," the tall copper haired woman said with a smile. "I'm Peaches. You know Hazel, and this is, Annabelle, Aspen, and the little one is Maisie." She flashed a wide, expectant smile. "We're here for you."

I frowned and loosened my grip on the knife.

"For me? Why?"

The only woman I knew was Hazel, and that was just barely. What business did they have with me?

"Word on the ranch is that you're getting married tomorrow."

Peaches folded her arms and all the others nodded, but the situation was tough to read.

"And you're here to warn me or what?"

Hazel laughed and shook her head, dark hair spilling over her shoulders.

"No, dummy, we came to help you out. Think of today as your bridal shower, bachelorette party, and dress fitting all in one."

"Plus rehearsal dinner," Peaches added with a grin. "Martha is so excited; she's already cooking up a feast for us for later."

She snapped her fingers and pushed inside, giving me no time to do anything but step aside.

"Damn it smells good in here," she groaned. "Are you cooking?"

"Breakfast," I answered automatically.

"Well we can take it with us back to the big house. Do you have anything you'll need before tomorrow?"

I stood rooted to the spot, mouth slightly open as if waiting for the words to come. "What?"

The dark haired woman with glasses let out a pretty, feminine laugh.

"Back down Peaches, give the woman a minute to catch up."

I sent her a grateful smile that she returned.

"We want to help you get ready for your big day and we're all set up at the Big House. How does that sound?"

Confusing. Suspicious. "Uhm, good?"

They all laughed, each woman wearing a knowing look like maybe they had the wrong idea.

"This isn't some love match. You all know that, right?"

The oven timer sounded, and the quiet, pregnant blonde finally spoke.

"I'll get it!"

I kept my eyes on her as she made her way to the kitchen and searched for oven mitts, which meant she hadn't been here before, a thought that provided me with far too much relief.

"You can tell this is Holden's baby because he goes crazy at the scent of meat."

She smiled but I felt all the blood drain from my face.

"Holden? Shit, I'm sorry about his face."

She held up a hand and laughed. "Don't worry about it. He told me the story, and I got a really good laugh. Did you really do it on purpose?"

Was this a trick? I nodded.

"I thought he was someone else."

Peaches wrapped an arm around me and sat me on the sofa. "We all came here for something else, mostly protection. Except AB." She sent a smile to the brunette in the red glasses. "But love was a byproduct, a happy one we like to think. Most of the time."

"Okay, that's great for you all, but that's not me and Cruz. We're practically strangers, but his mom said he might be able to help, and, well, I was desperate. But I'm not looking for love."

"Good," Hazel said, "because it found us when we weren't even looking for it. That makes it more exciting to watch, right girls?"

Each one nodded, wearing a wistful smile that made me wonder about their stories.

I shook my head at their smiles.

"This is a marriage of convenience. Nothing more. I don't even have a dress."

"We do, so let's wrap up that casserole because I call dibs on a big-ass piece," Peaches said with a nod towards Aspen. "

Grab anything you might need before the wedding tomorrow. Toothbrush, tampons, whatever. We leave in ten minutes."

I stared at Peaches, in awe of how all the women except Annabelle hopped up to do her bidding. She was like a bombshell drill sergeant with a sunshiny smile, and her orders didn't even seem like orders. More like favors.

"You're kind of scary, you know that?"

She nodded. "It's my superpower. That and my hacking abilities."

I didn't know if she meant computer or knife, so I nodded and went upstairs to repack my small bag. I took a few of those ten minutes for myself to calm my nerves and settle my emotions. These women, total strangers, had come to me and offered their help for my wedding. I didn't have relationships with any of them, yet they stepped in to perform the roles of best friends and family members. It was kind of overwhelming.

And really fucking sweet.

At the ten-minute mark, Peaches called out to me, and I grabbed my bag, slapped a smile on my face, and went with the women.

To my pre-wedding celebration.

How fucking weird was *that*?

Chapter Sixteen

Cruz

Today was the day I'd become a married man. To be honest, it wasn't a day I'd ever thought about, not in any real kind of way. Sure, I assumed I'd get married at some point, or maybe I just expected to eventually but never in real terms like this. The big patch of grass behind the big gleaming white house had been transformed with flowers and white chairs covered with red fabric. How two simple things could turn a field of green into a rainbow of vibrant colors was beyond me, but everyone had outdone themselves.

And they did it for me. Hennessy, too, but mostly for me.

I smiled and looked at the wooden archway covered in flowers and some kind of gauzy red fabric that gave it a romantic flair. The whole place looked perfect for a wedding, but it was meant for a real wedding, for two people who were in love and ready to pledge their lives to each other. And that wasn't me and Hennessy, but I couldn't shake the nerves that had gripped me since I woke up this morning.

Nerves. What the fuck do I have to be nervous about when this wasn't a real marriage? It was a temporary fix to a temporary problem. But no matter how many times I told myself that, I couldn't help the sense that this all felt pretty damn permanent. Maybe it was that whole *till death do us part* thing. Thinking about making Hennessy mine forever made me hot around the collar but also made my feet a little...*cold*.

I let out a long shaky breath and reminded myself that despite my nerves, I made a promise to Hennessy. And I wasn't a dude who went back on my promises. Ever.

"How you holdin' up?"

Holden's deep voice was a welcome respite from my thoughts.

"Nervous as fuck, but I'm just about sane again."

At least I was headed in that direction. Maybe.

"Marriage is some serious business, man."

I don't know how the hell the big silent cowboy knew my thoughts, but it was his superpower.

I turned away from all the flowers and looked over at Holden.

"Is that why you and Aspen haven't done it yet when you have a baby on the way?"

It was no secret he wanted to marry her, but the surprise was that she hadn't said yes. Yet.

Holden let out a deep rumbling laugh. "I would've married her the minute she said she loved me, but you know women, and Aspen is as girly as they come. She wants to wait until after the baby comes because she wants to look hot on our wedding night."

He laughed to himself as if recalling the conversation. "You think it matters if I tell her she's already hot or that I can't keep my hands off her?" He shook his head. "Nope. So, I'm waiting."

Dammit, that wasn't what I wanted to hear.

"Some best man you are," I grunted at him but Holden only laughed.

He clapped me on the back with a laugh. "I'm the perfect best man 'cause I'm gonna make sure you're there when Hennessy makes her big debut."

"You've seen her?"

She was gone when I got back yesterday with nothing but a note that the "girls" had come to get her and help with wedding details. I assumed that meant decorating, but now I wondered.

"You'll see her. Soon if we hurry." I followed Holden away from the big, shaded tree, and we made our way over to the cluster of chairs that weren't set up in the traditional two sides because the Reckless Bastards never did anything the normal way.

"Looks good."

"It does," I answered on a scratchy voice that was suddenly too dry to speak in full sentences.

Gunnar made his way over to where we stood, looking as dressed up as he ever would, trading his trademark black t-shirt for a short sleeve black button up with his regular uniform of jeans and shit kicker boots.

"Ready to get hitched to the old ball and chain?"

I laughed and arched a brow his way.

"Is that what you call Peaches?"

"Not to her face."

That had all three of us laughing as the rest of the women and the MC made their way to the chairs.

"Last chance to back out."

"I'm good," I told him and I realized the words were true. I was nervous but that was reasonable because this was marriage and it was a big fucking deal. It wasn't something I took lightly, and I would protect and care for Hennessy for as long as she was mine.

"Good," Holden leaned in and whispered, "because here she comes."

My gaze followed the path of Holden's index finger until I saw a vision of red and white. Hennessy walked slowly toward me looking hot as fuck in a white lace dress that highlighted every fucking curve she possessed. It nipped in at her waist, making her tits and her hips look like they'd give Marilyn Monroe a run for her money. But it was her creamy white skin that looked even starker with the red tendrils framing her face like a halo, or maybe it was the fire engine red lips that had my cock twitching in my pants. Then again, it could have been those red fucking stilettos that instantly had me imagining her, legs up, in nothing but those shoes.

"Watch out man, I think you're marrying the older, hotter sister of the fairy princess." Gunnar's voice was filled with amusement, and I knew he was having way too much fun at my expense.

"Shut up," I grunted, unable to tear my gaze away from Hennessy as she drew closer and closer. Her green eyes were filled with fear and wariness, but when she was just a few feet from me I saw something else. Anticipation.

TIED

Hennessy stopped about a foot from me, a nervous smile lighting up her face, but all I could focus on was those plump red lips.

"Hey," she said in a fragile voice.

"Hey," I told her, ignoring the breathless note in my voice. "You look beautiful."

The words tumbled out of my mouth just as I got my hands on her, pulling her by the waist until she was at my side and weaving our fingers together.

"Thanks," she said with a shy smile.

Her gaze darkened as she took in the sight of me in my black suit with the red tie as Peaches had demanded.

"You look pretty too," she said shyly.

Gunnar, along with everyone else enjoyed a good long laugh at her words. It relieved the tension between us, and when she squeezed my hand, I turned us both toward Gunnar.

Then, Hennessy and I got married.

The ceremony was short and sweet, just like our marriage would be.

Hopefully.

Chapter Seventeen

Hennessy

"You may now kiss the bride."

At Gunnar's words, both Cruz and I froze. Like idiots, we stood there with all of his closest friends watching us, staring at one another. The same uncertainty that churned in my gut swam in his eyes, which didn't make sense because Gunnar just told us exactly what to do.

Still, we stood there. Frozen.

"Uh," Gunnar cleared his throat, amusement sounding in that one drawn out syllable, "You may now *kiss* the bride." This time he spoke louder and slower, drawing another laugh from the crowd.

If that had been a real wedding meant to last forever, my heart would've soared at all the fun and laughter going on during the ceremony. It meant no one was taking themselves too seriously, that they were enjoying the moment without putting a lifetime of expectations on it. Since this was a marriage of convenience, it took the pressure off.

"Go on and kiss her, Uncle Cruz!" Maisie's laughter brought a smile to both our faces.

Smiles locked in place, we still stared at each other for another extended moment. The only thing I could think was, *shit*. Of all the things we'd talked about, our first—and only—kiss as a married couple was not one of them. But now the kiss was here and we were wholly unprepared.

"Uh, guys?" Holden's deep voice cut into my thoughts, and I sent him a grateful smile before leaning towards my now husband.

"I think they expect my husband to lay one on me." At my words, Cruz's gaze lasered in on my red painted lips that Peaches had spent five minutes on, insisting it would leave Cruz transfixed. I couldn't wait to tell her later, just how right she was. Then his gaze slid lower to my cleavage spilling over the top of the mermaid cut wedding dress, and he licked his lips. My breath hitched.

"If you won't kiss her, I will!"

That voice belonged to Slayer, the long haired dude I freaked out on that first night at The Barn Door.

Those words lit a fire under Cruz's ass, and he glared into the crowd until he found him.

"I can kiss my own damn wife, thank you very much."

Cruz's growl vibrated my whole body when he pulled me until our bodies were so close I could feel his heart beating against my chest. His body was big and hard, such a stark contrast to my smaller, softer frame. Big strong hands cupped my waist and slowly slid up my body. His fingers brushed along my ribcage and the edges of my breasts, and his hands slid up until one pressed dead center in my back and the other cupped my neck.

"Ready to be kissed like a proper wife?"

Hell, yeah. "Depends on how a proper husband kisses his wife. I've never been married before."

His lips curled into an amused grin, but the dark glint in his eyes told me he meant business. Before I could prepare myself for the feel of his lush lips on mine, they were there, soft and firm. Insistent. Greedy.

Cruz kissed like the devil, filling my entire body with a thick, heavy fire I couldn't control even if I wanted to. He kissed me like he'd been waiting his whole life to put his lips on me, for his tongue to slide against mine in an erotic dance that we both, somehow, knew the choreography to without one minute of practice. That moan was like a fucking rocket exploding inside of my body, heating me up until my blood flowed through me like lava.

The kiss was too intimate, too fucking erotic for a wedding. For a crowd full of well wishers whistling and clapping while we kissed like we were alone, because that's the kind of kiss it was. One that required privacy, intimacy for the things that came after a kiss like this, things like stripping each other naked and kissing every inch of skin on display. Things like a good, hard sweaty fuck. That thought brought me up short, and I pulled back, staring at him with wide eyed wonder.

"Wow."

One side of Cruz's mouth kicked up in an irresistible grin that hit me right between the thighs. Okay and maybe a little in the vicinity of my chest, but I was ignoring that and focusing solely on the desire coursing through my veins.

"You ain't seen nothin' yet, babe."

He pulled me close, so close that I could feel not only his heartbeat, but the huge cock growing in his pants. Then he dipped me over his forearm and pressed his lips to mine once again, and I lost all sense of time and place.

No man, no kiss had ever rendered me so powerless to my own desires. My arms tightened around his neck, and I pressed in closer, hungry to be as close to this man as I could, and still, it wasn't close enough. Cruz pulled back, a satisfied grin on his handsome face.

"Damn," I said in a hushed tone.

"Yeah, that's what I thought."

He clasped our hands together and lifted them in the air with a proud, wide smile, a move that was met with even louder cheers and whistles that I couldn't understand.

They all knew what this marriage was, and wasn't, but everyone smiled as if they're friend, their brother had found true love. We stopped long enough to take about thirty minutes' worth of photos before Cruz took me by the hand once again.

"Come on, wifey."

"Where are we going?"

Instead of answering, Cruz tugged me back up the aisle so fast I could barely keep up. It felt as if we walked forever thanks to the sexy but incredibly high red stilettos Peaches had insisted I wear. At the bottom of the back porch stairs he turned to me and bent down, scooping me in his arms.

"We're going to have a moment alone."

Alone? Instantly my nipples hardened, and I knew we'd both made a huge mistake here. A giant miscalculation, because this wasn't just a straightforward marriage to keep me safe from a crazy old mobster. Nope, it was a powder keg of lust and desire, threatening to blow up in our faces at any moment.

"We are?"

"Don't be scared, Hennessy. I'll only bite if you ask me to."

He winked and the tiny scrap of white lace I wore under the dress grew wetter by the second.

"I'm not scared," I insisted, but the truth was my heart raced like I was being chased by Eugene's thugs because the effect Cruz was having on me was impossible to explain. I wasn't the type of girl to lose her shit over a guy, no matter how gorgeous, how sexy, how fucking wet he made my panties. But here I was, *being* that girl.

"Good."

He carried me up the steps and inside the house where Martha was, once again, working furiously to make *her boys* happy.

"Smells divine, Miss Martha."

"Thanks, Cruz. The ceremony was beautiful and I think your bride will keep you in line." She turned to me with a gleam in her eyes and a wooden spoon in her hands. "Won't you?"

"I'll do my best," I told her, not wanting to see the light extinguish behind her eyes by telling her the truth.

"Go on, then. Get upstairs and help your bride get changed into something she can dance in."

His grin widened and those blue eyes turned to me, so close that I could see three different shades swimming in the depths.

"Yes ma'am."

For some reason, his grin did crazy things to my body, things I couldn't hide with him standing so close, doing his level best to keep me turned on.

"I'm perfectly capable of dressing and undressing myself," I told him as he took the stairs two at a time, as if I wasn't in his arms.

"Of course you can, babe, but it's my God given right as your husband to help you."

His lips twitched because even Cruz couldn't keep a straight face at that blatant lie.

"If that's all right with you," he added with a softer, sexier grin that only made me want to let him strip me down.

Why was I resisting this anyway? Cruz was delicious as hell and it was clear that he wanted me as badly as I wanted him, and there was the small fact that he was now my husband.

But did I really want our first time to be rushed with two dozen people outside, getting ready for a big-ass party? No, I didn't. But I wasn't prepared to shut the door on the possibility of us. Together. Naked.

"Well, the zipper on this dress is a bit tricky."

"Fuck me," he growled when we finally made it to the room Peaches and the girls had converted into a bridal suite for the day. There was white silk and lace everywhere, and a bucket of champagne chilling beside the bed.

"Don't tease me, Hennessy."

"I'm not," I told him and let my body slide down his, feeling every hard muscle before my feet hit the ground. I took a step back, my heart thudding in my chest as I twirled to give him my back.

"It's hidden between the seams in the middle." My breath hitched as his knuckles brushed against the bare skin of my back when his fingers gripped the zipper.

"Be gentle. Please."

A big puff of breath whooshed from him, heating my skin even more, and then he tugged the zipper, slowly until the cool air on my back made me shiver. "Holy fuck, Hennessy."

A smile touched my lips at the guttural, primal sound that dripped from his lips. I took my time, shoving the fabric over my hips and letting it fall to the ground. I turned, slowly, my gaze focused on the way his eyes moved as he took in every detail. The white lace-up corset with matching lace thong were too sexy all on their own, but Aspen had insisted the garter belts and lace-top stockings would blow his mind.

She wasn't wrong. The look in his eyes made me feel like an incredibly sexy woman who was desirable. Lusted after. I stood a little taller, shoving my chest out just a little bit more.

"Thanks for your help, Cruz."

His eyes darkened to jet black and he licked his lips, making my nipples pebble beneath the bra.

"Fuck!" Cruz growled again, the sound dark and foreboding as he took a step back. And then another. Then, shock of all shocks, he turned on his heels, yanked the door open and walked out.

Happy fucking wedding day to me.

Chapter Eighteen

Cruz

Even though the sun had set long ago, I could still hear the sounds of music coming from the big house. Hennessy and I left the festivities about an hour ago, but there had been no signs of the party stopping anytime soon.

I couldn't say I blamed them. The MC had been through some shit over the past few months, hell the past few years, and it was about time we had a reason to party. Technically, the wedding was the reason for the party, but it served as a celebration of Stone's birth, Peaches' safe return, the death of Farnsworth, and all the other shit that had been thrown at us lately. We had plenty of reasons to celebrate, and I knew they'd be drinking and smoking and partying until the sun came up.

Hennessy didn't say much on the short ride back to my cabin. Our cabin, now. The truth was she hadn't said much to me aside from, "I'll be in my room," when we first got back. I couldn't blame her though, after the way I walked out on her in the bridal suite. It was a pussy move. I knew that the moment I walked out, but dammit, the way she looked in all that white lace was more than I could handle.

She was all creamy soft skin, freckles and curves, standing there in front of me wearing virginal white and a sultry smile on her face. Virginal and innocent really wasn't my fucking thing, but holy fucking hell did my hands itch—even now—to touch her.

She looked hotter than hell standing there with her tits poking out, cleavage spilling over the top and a flirty grin on her face. I wanted her, badly, and in that bridal suite I could have torn that delicate fabric from her body and fucked her until we both couldn't move. Except I didn't do pity fucks. I wanted Hennessy, and I wanted her to come to me because she wanted to ride my cock, not because she felt like she owed me for marrying her. Protecting her.

TIED

I poured another shot of Remy down my throat and glared out at the starry fucking night, feeling fuzzy but nowhere close to drunk. Pissed off and horny too, but none of that mattered. Not tonight and probably not any other night either, which meant I was about to reacquaint my hand and my cock because every time I closed my eyes there she was, in white lingerie, white stockings, and hot as fuck red heels.

The next shot of Remy went down easier, and I closed my eyes to let the room temperature amber liquid seep into my veins, warm me up, and make everything a little bit fuzzier. There she was again, taunting me. Teasing me.

"Drinking alone?"

Hennessy's husky voice behind me came out of nowhere, and I cursed myself for not being more aware of my surroundings. She wasn't my real fucking wife. She needed me to keep her safe, and I couldn't do that if I was too busy picturing myself sliding my dick inside her.

"Yep. Want some?"

I held the bottle up without looking at her, because I couldn't, and she surprised me by taking the bottle from my hand. I listened as she took two big sips and handed it back to me.

"Thanks. I prefer it on the rocks, though." There was humor in her voice, and I chanced a glance at her over my shoulder

"Goddammit."

I really should have listened to my instinct and kept my eyes on the twinkling stars above or the expansive flat land of Hardtail Ranch bathed in moonlight. She was no longer dressed up in the virginal wedding lingerie from earlier.

Oh fuck no.

Instead, Hennessy had changed into red. Fiery, flaming red that made her skin look paler and her hair look like it had been kissed by fire. The white corset was gone, replaced by one of those sexy ass negligees that hugged her curves and drew my attention to the patch of red between her legs.

"What the fuck?"

My cock was hard instantly and all the peace of mind I'd been working to build flew out the damn window.

She blinked innocently, like she didn't understand. Her lush mouth was fixed in a rounded 'O' that had my cock straining against my zipper to slide between those lips.

"Excuse me?"

That was anger, which I could deal with better than the hurt or sadness I expected.

"What are you wearing?"

"Pajamas," she bit out through clenched teeth. "This shouldn't bother you at all, Cruz."

I turned away from her, unable to look at her another second without forgetting that I didn't want a pity fuck. I wanted a hard, sweaty fuck that had her screaming my name and begging for more.

"Yeah, why's that?"

"Because you walked away earlier. I was standing there in sexy lingerie with a wet pussy thanks to you and you just walked away."

The sound of her heels told me she was calling my bluff, and she did, taking the seat right beside me and crossing her legs, making it impossible to ignore her.

"Are you a tease or something, Cruz?"

I heard the challenge in her voice and turned to her with a raised eyebrow. "A tease?"

She nodded. "You did your best to make me want you and then you walked away. So Cruz, I have to ask, what the fuck?"

I hadn't expected her to call me out like this, but I should have. I didn't know Hennessy and treating her like she was every other woman wasn't going to make living together any easier.

"Did I bruise your ego, Hen?"

She barked out a laugh and stood, leaning against the pine bannister I spent hours cutting and sanding myself, crossing her legs at the ankle so my gaze was drawn to the red fabric covering her pussy. "Did you bruise my...are you an idiot or are you just cruel? Did you get me all riled up just to prove to yourself you could?"

I stared at her for a long time, unsure if I should feel offended that she thought so little of me or pissed off she called me an idiot.

"Well? Answer me, dammit. I can handle rejection, Cruz, and if that's what this is, just fucking say it."

Arms folded over her chest, making her cleavage look even more spectacular, she waited. Impatiently.

"I don't want you to fuck me because you think you have to."

She laughed again and this time it was soft and sexy and feminine.

"I don't *have* to fuck anyone, Cruz. Ever."

"Still," I grunted and took another swig, or two, of Remy.

"Oh, bullshit. Look at me." She extended her arms out to either side of her body and stood straight, less than a foot from me, making sure I took in every detail of her body. I looked my fill until her words brought my attention back to her face.

"You think I'd wear this for obligatory sex? No, I'd wear nothing at all. I'm trying to turn you the fuck *on* Cruz, but I guess it's not working."

Just like that, all the fire, the piss and vinegar, fled. Like she was just done. Hennessy shrugged her shoulders and walked away, giving me one final dagger in the heart when I caught sight of her round, meaty ass cheeks, bare, with nothing but a red triangle for decoration.

I was on my feet in a flash, just inside the front door of my cabin, grabbing her arm before she could get too far from me. I pulled her until her chest slammed into mine, smiling at the feel of those diamond-hard nipples against my chest.

"No more fucking talking, Hen."

Just in case she thought about using that pretty little mouth for anything but pleasure for the rest of the night, I crashed my lips down against hers, devouring the taste of Hennessy and Remy, my two favorite drinks, on my tongue.

She didn't put up a fight, giving in instantly. I smiled against her mouth because I enjoyed a woman that didn't pretend she was too good for a good hard fuck, and Hen knew that's exactly what she was about to get. She slid one hand down to squeeze my ass and the fingers of her other hand curled around the back of my neck, giving it a gentle tug. She moaned into my mouth and tried to get closer.

That was all I needed to push her deeper into the living room, kicking the door shut behind me to close out the world, even though the party music provided a quiet, distant soundtrack. My mouth never left hers, though, taming and teasing her with my kisses until she was putty in my hands.

"Fuck," she said on a breathless sigh when she pulled back, looking at me like I was some magical fucking creature she didn't recognize.

"Right?" I answered. My mouth was on hers again even as my hands roamed her body in search of how to get the damn lingerie off those sweet curves.

"The back," she panted and kissed her way from my mouth down my neck before she sank her teeth in to the muscle between my neck and shoulder.

My hands flew to the back, and I smiled when I found a dozen little hooks. I grabbed it with both hands and pulled it apart until the fabric tore and fell to the ground. Hennessy gasped, but it was a sound of desire, not shock, and that sound hit me right in the cock.

"Better," I growled and dropped to my knees, grabbing the tiny red band at her hips and tugged it down. Slowly, until she shivered in my hands.

"Too. Slow."

TIED

I let out a low chuckle at her words, but this was my show. I was in charge of her pleasure, and that's just how it fucking was. "I could go slower."

Her hand started a path down her chest to her belly. "I could just get started on my own."

"You could," I told her and grabbed her wrist to stop her movement. "But then you'd miss out on all the fun." Her pussy pulsed at my words, that pink swollen clit poking out of her pussy lips made my lips water, and I blew on her.

"Oh!"

Yeah, that was much better. The scent of her arousal had me hard as a fucking rock, but I wasn't ready to unleash my cock. Yet. First, I needed to teach Hennessy a little lesson.

"Stay just like that," I told her as I spread her legs wider than shoulder width apart and slid beneath her.

"Like this?"

I nodded and stuck my tongue out, letting the tip tease her clit until she shivered and tossed her head back. Her pussy was fat and slick, exactly how I liked it, and I ate her like she was my last fucking meal, lapping up all the juices as they dripped from her cunt. Hennessy looked down at me and grabbed a handful of my hair, her eyes dark with desire, focused on her orgasm that was *just* out of reach.

"Oh fuck! Cruz!" Her hips began to move back and forth, right over the center of my tongue, faster and faster as she chased down her pleasure. "Oh fuck! Yes!"

Now this was exactly the kind of dirty talk I loved when I had a naked woman with me. She was wild and out of control with desire, ready to come. But not yet. I let my tongue slip inside her wet hot pussy, groaning when her juices coated my tongue and the scent of her hit my nose.

"Fuck," I groaned, knowing the muffled sound would vibrate her clit.

"Cruz!" She moved faster and faster, gripping my hair so fucking tight it brought a tear to my eye and my cock almost erupted. Then she went still for half a beat before her body trembled with the force of her orgasm, violent convulsions exploding out of her.

"Oh, fuck, Cruz, yes!" She shouted her enjoyment and came all over my face, her honeyed juices dripping down my throat so sweet and thick I thought I might blow my load right then and there in my pants.

My tongue slowed, letting her ride out her pleasure until it was too much, then I licked her for another full minute or two just so she knew who was in charge.

"I'd say that's a good start, wouldn't you, *wifey*?"

A laugh erupted out of her and another aftershock rocked her that only made her laugh harder.

"Holy fuck, it was a *damn good* start."

"Exactly what I wanted to hear," I said and got to my feet. I wasn't even standing for a full second before Hennessy's mouth was on mine, devouring it like her favorite flavor in the world was her pussy on my tongue. I totally fuckin' dug it. She kissed me wildly, not giving a damn when her teeth clashed against mine, just laughed and kept going while her hands made quick work of what was left of my wedding clothes.

Hennessy took my cock in her hand and stroked, gently at first and then she added more pressure and speed until I was hard and dripping with pre-come.

"Bigger than I imagined," she purred and kissed me again.

That was all it took for my control to snap, Hennessy telling me she thought about my cock. I pushed her against the wall with a growl and took my cock in my hand, lowering my mouth to get a taste of one of those juicy nipples. Her head fell back and her back arched towards me, offering more of her juicy titties.

"Oh, fuck!" The words came out on a whisper and I was ready to take her.

"You're good with that mouth," she told me when I released her with a pop.

"I'm good with this too," I told her, stroking my cock and enjoying the way her eyes glazed over at the sight. I lifted her into the air and lowered her until she was impaled on my cock.

"Oh fucking shit," she wailed.

I smiled at her words with clenched teeth as her tight cunt clamped around my cock so hard I didn't think I'd make it a full fucking minute inside of her.

Her big ass fit in my hands perfectly. I could just raise her up and lower her down on my cock like a fiery little fuck doll. Over and over I did just that, enjoying the savage sounds of pleasure she made while I fucked her.

"Oh," she began and let her head fall back with a loud thud against the wall. "Ouch," she said with a laugh.

"Careful, babe, this cock comes with a warning label."

She laughed out loud at that even as she reached out to grip my shoulders when I held her against the wall and pounded into her tight, wet cunt. "Yeah? Prove it."

I focused on that twinkle in her green eyes while I fucked her, hard and fast, until sweat slicked both of our bodies. Until it was difficult to hold on to her slick flesh while I pounded into her, over and over, her crazed sounds driving me out of my fucking mind.

Hennessy, hot fuck that she was, held a tit out to me and I took it, sucking and biting hard while I plowed into her pussy with the force of a jackhammer.

"Oh fuck. Oh fuck. Oh fuck!"

I smiled when her pussy clenched tight around me, her second orgasm barreling down on her and coating my cock with her juices. "Come for me, babe. Come all over my cock."

"Make me," she shot back with attitude and a sexy, sleepy smile that said she was already more than satisfied.

I gripped her ass and pounded into her pussy, hard and deep, letting my middle finger slide just inside her asshole. She was tight, untested based on the way she pulsed around my finger.

TIED

"Cruz...oh fu-uck!" Hennessy falling apart wasn't just a beautiful fucking sight with her head tilted back, eyes closed and a perfect cock-sized O shaping her mouth.

Her orgasm came hard and fast, triggering my own and milking me dry until my legs trembled.

"Oh, God. Hennessy!" Her name roared out of my mouth as I pounded into her, letting my come fill her until we both collapsed in a heap on the wooden floor right there in the living room.

A nervous laugh escaped, and she looked down at me with an exhausted smile as her pussy clenched my cock one last time before he slipped from her body.

"I propose we do that at least once every damn day."

Her wide grin left me transfixed and I was already hooked on her sex, her responsiveness, and the way she went all in where pleasure was concerned.

"If you think you can handle it."

I was already planning how I would fuck her later that night.

TIED

Chapter Nineteen

Hennessy

There was something about waking up with a pair of big strong arms wrapped around me that made me feel decidedly feminine. I wasn't the kind of chick who got all gooey over guys, and I wasn't easily swayed by pretty words, but give me a few orgasms and a nice rock hard furnace to sleep against, and I was putty in his hands.

My eyes fluttered open, adjusting to the first rays of sun that filtered in through the blinds Cruz rarely closed. It took a moment to adjust, but I turned in Cruz's arms so I could get a real, unguarded look at him. The man was so fucking beautiful that I swear to God it made my pussy ache to look at him. He had Esme's honey-brown skin but most of his features from his impossibly blue eyes to his nose, his strong jawline and wide mouth paired with full lips all came from his dad. Even asleep and vulnerable, he was painfully beautiful.

Not just beautiful, either. Cruz was a goddamn work of art. Pornographic art, if my body's reaction to his sleeping form was any indication. My nipples pebbled against his chest, and I had to squeeze my thighs shut against the hard, thumping pulse between my legs. My body wanted more of what it got last night, namely so much pleasure that I had an out of body experience when Cruz coaxed a fifth orgasm from me.

The man had a talented mouth. A very talented cock. Incredibly talented hands. And fingers. And that tongue. No man had ever given my pussy so much attention with his mouth, and I'm pretty sure he turned me into an addict.

But last night hadn't been enough, not for me anyway. We'd done so much, to and for each other, but there was more, and dammit I wanted it. Badly.

Cruz stirred, but he never woke, pulling my body flush against his hard, sculpted muscles and wrapping his arms around me tightly. It was oddly protective, made even more so by the fact that he was more asleep than awake. Instantly, my attention was stolen by the feel of his semi-hard cock nudging against my already swollen clit. I sucked in a breath and let it out slowly as the devil struck me with an idea. Slowly, I wiggled in Cruz's arms until his grip loosened enough to put a few inches of space between us.

Tugging on the blanket, I let my gaze wander over every smooth inch of skin revealed to me. He had a few tattoos, some from his time in the Army, like names and dates of fallen friends on his back shoulder, while others were more personal like the Virgin Mary-looking tattoo on his arm. But my absolute favorite tat was the strip of words across his Adonis belt. *War always costs more than you expect.* I didn't want to feel sorry for him, not when my body was on fire for him, but dammit that quote said there was more to him than his sexy, goofy persona.

A fact I had no business thinking about. We'd been married less than twenty-four hours and good sex, incredible sex, didn't change that, so I turned my attention back to what mattered. His gorgeous body and the way it felt on my lips as I kissed my way down his body.

Still more asleep than awake, Cruz moaned. I felt bold and insanely horny as images from last night blended with the sight of his body, specifically his cock. Even close up he had a pretty cock, light tan with a pink tip, it was long and thick and reminded me of a lollipop. He wasn't too thick, but just thick enough that sucking him off was slightly uncomfortable in my mouth. That discomfort only made it hotter, especially when I thought about how close he'd been to blowing when I blew him last night, but he shoved me over the edge of the sofa and fucked me doggystyle. It was hard and fast, and I came in less than two minutes.

Now though, I was determined to see what he tasted like. All of him. I held the base of his cock in one hand, enjoying the way it shot straight up like a skyscraper, holding firm as I licked my way around it with a moan. One little drop of liquid beaded at the slit and the tip of my tongue landed on it, rubbing it in before licking it off and taking all of him in my mouth.

"Oh fuck!" Cruz shot straight up, sending his cock so deep in my throat I nearly choked and the tightening around his head sent him falling back onto the pillows.

"Fuck!" he moaned. His hips slowly rolled in a circle like he was trying really hard not to fuck my mouth.

When he lost the battle and straight up thrust down my throat, I smiled around his cock and took him as deep as I could until my eyes watered.

"Oh fuck, Hen! Fuck!" He said that word, over and over, panting it like it was the only word that made sense to him. I wasn't gonna lie, those primal, guttural songs hit me right in the lady parts with a swell of feminine pride.

"Hen," he said, this time the word was filled with reverence.

I closed my eyes and licked and sucked, sucked hard and slow, fast and then slow, deep and slow. Every way I could think of until his fingers speared through my hair so he could hold me right where he wanted me, and his hips thrust, sending his cock deeper down my throat. I moaned and took him even deeper, my pussy getting wetter with arousal.

Cruz was lost, crazy with desire when I looked up at him. His gaze was on my face as he pumped into my mouth, watching my every move. It was exhilarating, terrifying, and intoxicating all at once. Another moan escaped my lips when he pulled out, and my eyes went wide, hungry with want.

Cruz slipped between my lips again, on a long deep thrust, and he was gone.

"Oh fuck, Hennessy!" His hands tightened in my hair as his body convulsed, jerking this way and that while his hot come slid down my throat. Every jerking thrust sending another salty drop down my throat.

"Oh fuck, yes! Baby, fuck...yes!" He froze, his cock as deep in my throat as it could get. A growl tore through the air that told me he was well beyond the ability to control himself.

I swallowed, teasing him and hungry to see more signs of him losing control.

"Hen," he growled as his fingertips tightened on my scalp, his cock sliding slowly in and out of my mouth like it was my pussy. His gaze seared through me, holding me in its grip, so I had no choice to but watch as his eyes darkened and his abs tightened when another, smaller spasm tore through him. I collapsed between his thighs, his cock still between my lips.

I released him with a pop that made his body shudder. "Wow."

Cruz chuckled and propped up on his elbows so he could get a better look at me. I gripped his cock in my hand and licked the red, sensitized tip with a smile.

"Makes me happy knowing how good I made you feel. Knowing it was my mouth making you crazy like that."

His gaze darkened and his hands reached for me, gripping my upper arms to pull me up the length of his body. And then his lips crashed against mine, kissing me long and hard until I was breathless. And wet again, pressing up against him like a dog in heat.

"Good to know," he said. His hand landed hard on my ass, and he smiled at the gasp that escaped.

"Yeah?"

He nodded. "Oh yeah. Because I can't wait to return the favor." Then he kissed me and slowly slid me down the length of his cock. I rode him hard until we both passed out once again, in each other's arms.

Chapter Twenty

Cruz

I couldn't stop smiling. It wasn't normally something I would complain about, smiling too much wasn't even in my five-year plan after spending almost a decade sleeping in a war zone, but here I was, married for just over a week, and I was smiling like a pussy-whipped fool. And it was all my wife's fault. Specifically, it was her mouth that was to blame. Her sweet, plump lips and that warm tongue loved to cradle the weight of my cock. Yeah, her penchant for wake up blow jobs was definitely to blame for the stupid fucking smile on my face.

"I guess marriage agrees with you." Slayer's appearance at my side and his words reminded me where I was. At The Barn Door, where I should be working, not fantasizing about my wife's hot little mouth. I didn't miss the amusement in Slayer's voice, I simply ignored it.

But I thought about his words and shrugged. "It's not what I thought it would be, and not just because of the circumstances, but it's not bad." That was the fucking understatement of the year. I thought we'd pass the time in polite distance, trying hard not to get in each other's way, not spending every night making each other come.

"She insists on cooking, which I don't mind because it's damn nice to come home to a hot meal every damn day. Nothing against steak and potatoes but it's nice to have enchiladas, burgers, mac & cheese. Hell, she even made curry if you can believe it." And she'd served it in nothing but a deep blue negligee and no panties. But I wasn't gonna tell him that.

Slayer snorted a laugh and folded his arms over his chest, looking straight ahead at the crowd on the main floor, dancing and fucking like it was the end of the world. "My invite must've gotten lost in the mail," he mused with a smile on his face. "Either that or you're too busy keeping your wife barefoot and naked to think about your poor starving friend."

TIED

"Starving my ass. Didn't I see you letting Beat choke on your dick a few days ago?" It was the perfect distraction because I didn't want to talk about the fact that he was dead fucking on. I had done my best to keep Hennessy naked and sated and boneless from coming so much. When we were home together, I fucked her. I ate her pussy or licked her asshole. Finger fucked her while we watched TV or just play with her pussy while we watched the sun set. I was a man addicted to my new wife.

"It's like that, huh?" Slayer's amusement had grown ten-fold which made me think I'd missed something daydreaming about Hennessy. "Well, I'm happy for you."

"You got a master class blowjob from a world class freak and you're jealous of me?" I shook my head and let out a derisive snort. "It's a marriage of convenience and it's just sex," I insisted even though the words felt wrong on my tongue. Sometimes Hennessy got this look in her green eyes that made me wonder if she was starting to get ideas, but she hadn't said anything so neither had I.

"Whatever you say, man."

"It is," I foolishly insisted, glaring hard at my brother, but it only made the fucker laugh harder.

"Good. Then you won't be bothered when I tell you that she went downstairs with a Caligula basket about two minutes ago."

The laughter in his voice was a living, breathing thing, and it followed me as I took off down the stairs to figure out which orgy room she was headed to. The basket was my own fucking brain child. Obsessed with history, I knew the rich members would get a kick out of a golden basket filled with booze, condoms, caramel, strawberry glaze, chocolate, whipped cream and other things perfect for licking off body parts.

I found her in the leather orgy room, dressed up like a little redheaded cowgirl, sexy as fuck in the tiniest Daisy Dukes I'd ever seen. Hennessy laughed and flirted easily with the customers, always making sure they had a good time without becoming *part* of the good time.

"Enjoy," she offered with a smile and took a few steps back and out of sight.

I watched Hennessy as she watched them, noting the way her breath hitched and her nipples hardened beneath that plain white tank top that did dangerous things for her luscious tits. Her mouth was open slightly and the pulse at the base of her neck raced faster as she got more and more turned on.

"Who are you watching?" I whispered the words in her ear, satisfied when she let out another startled gasp.

But then, Hennessy leaned into me and licked her lips. "The two women sharing a cock."

I found them easily, smiling at the way she couldn't look away. "You want to share my cock with another woman?" The idea had me hard as a rock, and I wondered if she was that kind of girl.

"No. Maybe. Maybe I just like the idea of turning it into a game, to see how much pleasure you can take or which of us can make you come first. That could be kind of hot."

The longing in her voice made me wish we were anywhere but at work.

One hand pressed flat against her belly, and I tugged her back against my cock.

"You had me at four lips and two tongues on my cock." I ground against her ass and smiled against her neck when she shuddered against me.

"He does look pretty damn pleased," she said as she slid a hand between us and curled it around my cock, stroking me through my jeans. "So, so pleased." Her voice was low and deep, thick with desire.

A throat cleared behind us, and I knew it was Slayer, but still I turned to verify. He gave a brief nod and disappeared. Shit. "Gotta go."

I stepped back but Hennessy's hand curled into my shirt, keeping me right there with her soft curves in my hands.

"Tonight, I'm thinking sixty-nine. Whoever comes first has to take orders. Sex slave. All night."

I groaned and leaned in for another kiss, unable to believe this fake marriage had already been so much fun.

"Deal," I told her and took off with a limp, forcing my mind to cite military code to get rid of my boner.

"What's up?"

Slayer stood at the top of the stairs, his gaze scanning the room on a nonstop swivel.

"Peaches called Gunnar with some intel from the twins at the B&B. Two newcomers in town, they said. Turns out they're McArthur's men."

"Fuck." They were already in town which meant we were already two steps behind. I guess this was where my bubble—filled with homecooked meals and fucking each other hard and fast and on top of and up against every flat surface we could find—burst.

Chapter Twenty-One

Hennessy

"Where in the hell have you been?"

The anger in Cruz's deep voice pulled me from my thoughts and brought me up short. The path to his cabin from the main entrance of Hardtail Ranch was close to a mile, and I used that time to get my thoughts straight. Peaches had insisted on coming with me to pick up the marriage certificate.

She was weird and standoffish the entire time so when we got back to the ranch, I was happy to have the peace and quiet the long walk provided me.

"I was out," I told him easily, not bothering to look up to confirm the tone of his voice.

"That's not fucking good enough, Hennessy."

I sighed, wondering if this was where he got all possessive and abusive on me. I wasn't so high and mighty that I couldn't admit Cruz wouldn't be the first man in my life to show his true colors too soon, but his one-eighty threw me for a loop.

"That's too bad, Cruz. You don't own me."

"I don't own...are you fucking kidding me?"

At his incredulous tone, I did look up just in time to see him shake his head, an incoherent sound coming from his thick lips.

"I'm not trying to *own* you; I'm trying to keep you safe. Like you asked me to do!"

Okay, so he had me there.

"Fine, Peaches and I went into town to pick up our marriage certificate."

I pulled the plastic-covered document from the tote bag on my shoulder and showed it to him.

"Figured if I sent it to Homer, this might put a quick end to things."

Cruz wasn't just a pretty face. Nope, he was smart as hell, too, and he missed nothing.

"A quick end to what things, Hennessy? Did something happen?"

I sighed and leaned against the sturdy porch.

"Not really, no. It's just that I've had this weird feeling for the past few days, like I'm being watched. I know it's crazy, and it's probably one of your MC guys, but I felt it even more today."

I shivered at the memory. "Maybe I've been stuck on the ranch so long that normal human interaction scares me now." I let out a bitter laugh but Cruz wasn't having it.

He took the bag from my shoulder and set it beside the door, nodding for me to take a seat in one of the chairs on the front porch.

"We got some intel that says a few of McArthur's men are in Opey. They've been asking questions."

His words hit me like a ton of bricks. While I've been over here acting like a silly fucking housewife, cooking up homemade meals and fucking like I had any ownership of this man, Eugene's men were closing in. But something else niggled at me, how calm Cruz was.

"How long have they been in town?" I don't know what possessed me to ask the question, but the moment I did, I knew.

"A week or so," he said with a casual shrug, like it wasn't a big fucking deal.

"Why didn't you tell me?" I felt my anger rising, and I tried to keep it in check, since he was doing me a really big fucking favor and all.

"I didn't want you to freak out." Again with the calm and cool tone, like I was a frightened pet he had to coax into the warm house. "I was afraid you might do something stupid like run off without telling me. Or worse, confront them."

"I wouldn't," I insisted even in the face of his incredulous expression. "I wouldn't."

"Not even to gloat that you won by getting married and away from McArthur?"

How in the hell? I gasped.

"Okay maybe it would have been a little gloating but only in a text and only to Homer."

And that wasn't even the fucking point, was it?

"What else do I need to know?"

"Nothing. You're safe, and that's what matters."

"Now who's fucking kidding who? I went into town today, Cruz, completely oblivious that Eugene's men were so close. I want to know what's going on in my life, Cruz." That was a non-starter as far as I was concerned.

He sighed, blue eyes staring a hole in my forehead. "Thank you would have worked better than all of this bull shit," he said, his voice angry. Ice cold.

"Thanks," I shouted back, sarcastic as ever. "Just don't keep shit from me."

When Cruz hit me with that nonchalant stare again, I lost it and got in his face.

He stepped away and shook his head but I was there, right back in his face. Spoiling for a fight. "You want to do this now?"

He cocked a brow at me and I nodded, ready to let him have it.

"Good," he said.

He knelt down and tossed me over his shoulder.

"What the hell do you think you're doing? Put me down!" He did. Eventually. Tossing me onto the back seat of the four wheeler.

"We're doing this, apparently."

"Where are we going?"

Cruz cast a quick look over his shoulder. "No talking," he said and started the engine, leaving me to keep arguing and risk falling off, or wrapping my arms around his hard body and temporarily forget why we were fighting.

He pulled to a stop in front of The Barn Door, which oddly enough looked like little more than one of many farm buildings in the cold, harsh light of day. I couldn't speak as we entered, not when he took my hand and clasped it with his and not when he led me downstairs to one of the private rooms.

The room was done up in red and blue and purple silk and satin, like some sex room in a middle eastern palace. The colors were erotic and soothing at the same time and instantly my pulse kicked up.

"Get naked," he barked at me.

I stared at him for a long moment and then found my fingers working quickly to do his bidding. I peeled off every stich of clothing until I stood in the middle of the room, bed on one side and a wall full of toys on the other, stark naked.

"And?"

"Lie on the bed." His back was still to me, and Cruz was fully dressed, but that only amped up my arousal. My nipples were hard as rocks and my pussy clenched and ached as I climbed on top of the high, oversized black steel frame bed.

"Good girl," he groaned and got busy tying each of my limbs to a corner of the bed. Leather straps softened with a fur lining felt erotic against my overheated skin.

"Too bad you can't always be so good." He tightened the straps at my wrist and looked at my tits, heat darkening his eyes to damn near black. "You said you wouldn't question me," he grumbled and fastened my left leg and then my right to the bed, giving each one an extra tug.

"You're safe."

"I know," I told him, my heart thudding against my rib cage. "But I have a right to know."

Cruz nodded and ran one finger from my ankle all the way up to the top of my thigh until one knuckle grazed my clit.

"You make me crazy, Hennessy."

I rolled my eyes at his growly words, but secretly, I was thrilled. It wasn't often I made a guy lose his good sense.

"And now I think it's time I returned the favor."

Before I could ask Cruz what he meant by that, his lips grabbed my clit and slurped, sending a tidal wave of vibrations through my body.

"So good."

A slow grin spread across his face. Cruz licked me in slow, gentle strokes before he slipped his tongue inside my pussy. My eyes slid shut and my back arched as much as it could with the restraints. That was when I heard the telltale buzz of a motor. My eyes flew open and looked down at Cruz, tongue deep in my pussy with a vibrating bullet pressed firmly against my clit.

It was too much. It wasn't enough, either, but mostly it was too much, sending shivers racing up and down my sweat-slicked skin. My nipples were so hard they ached, and my pussy leaked so much, I felt embarrassment trying to creep into the moment.

"Cruz." His name came out on a strangled cry, and he smiled, his eyes never leaving mine. "Please."

He chuckled and another lightning bolt of pleasure shot through me, but there was nothing I could do about it. I couldn't reach for him, couldn't touch him and urge him on. The fact that I couldn't do what I wanted only made me hotter, made me want to come more.

But the more I tried to reach for it, the more Cruz kept it out of my reach. So I gave in, enjoying the way his finger fucked me while the bullet pleased me until my eyes crossed. I cried real tears when he tossed the bullet aside and made love to my clit while two fingers pumped in and out of me, sending a rush of liquid out of me on the third orgasm.

"Cruz, please."

"Please, what?" He licked me again, right across my pussy.

"Tell me, Hennessy." The tip of his tongue flicked my clit. "Tell me what you want."

He was teasing me beyond all reason, and I could barely breathe or see straight. I didn't even have enough oxygen to speak. "You. I want your cock. I need it." He'd made me come every way imaginable, and still my pussy wanted more. It had to be him. "Please, Cruz. Fuck me."

He let out a growl, and moments later I felt the restraints loosen on my legs and his big body was there, his cock teasing my clit and my opening until unintelligible groans slipped from my lips. His cock invaded my cunt, thick and hard and determined to fuck me to within an inch of my life. I watched his face, twisted in beautiful agony as he thrust in and out of me.

"Yes! Oh fuck yes!" Harder and harder he slammed into me and that was it, exactly what I needed to give me one final push over the edge. I flew apart into a billion tiny shards of pleasure, every piece vibrating as if becoming one with the universe. His hips bucked harder and harder and then they stilled, tiny vibrating shocks shook his body as his orgasm flooded out of him and straight into me.

It was more explosive than I could have imagined. More intoxicating than Texas moonshine, more addictive than any drug, Cruz had me firmly under his spell.

By the time he freed my hands and took me back to the cabin, I could barely walk and couldn't even remember what we were fighting about.

Chapter Twenty-Two

Cruz

"Hey. Where the hell are you?" I said into the phone. I didn't mean to come off sounding like some jealous asshole, but Hennessy had been gone for more than an hour, and I was antsy as fuck. She laughed and the sound in my ear was sweet and husky, the rush of blood to my cock was almost enough to make me forget. Almost. "Well?"

She laughed again. "I'm busy working. What are *you* doing?"

Working was right. For the past few days she'd been helping me work on planning the party that was supposed to help The Barn Door members forget that a dude had shot his fucking brains out where they fuck.

The truth was that Hennessy was doing most of the work, and she was doing a damn good job. "I'm waiting on you so we can both get to work. What's taking so long?"

"Regretting giving the old wifey a little freedom?" She asked.

Hell yes. "Not at all. Just concerned is all." It went against my better judgment to let her go out on her own, but after days of her giving me shit, I let her go, and it wasn't sitting well with me. At all.

"Are you on your way home?" Home. Was that what this was for her?

"Yes. And I found the perfect party favors for the guests. That's why I was gone longer than we agreed."

At least her tone was apologetic, but I would rather she was already on the ranch.

"Wait until you see them. They're already in the trunk to keep them safe from the heat and the small town gossip."

"Safe from the heat? You know there's still a full week until the party, right?"

"Yep. I already called Aspen, and she's letting me store them in her and Holden's deep freezer."

"You've been busy." She was supposed to go into town to pick up the handwritten invitations and decorations and that was it.

"I could have gone with you to do this."

"Yes but that would be the same as me staying at the ranch wouldn't it?"

Damn frustrating woman. "You're making me crazy Hen, and not in a good way." Keeping her safe was my job, dammit, and it was hard to do when she was miles away in town. "Come home."

She laughed. "I'm on my way to the car now. I promise I'm taking this serious Cruz. I've been watching my back and clocking all the cars I see. So far, there have been no repeats and no creepers."

"That you've seen."

"Yes." She sighed her frustration. "None that I've seen. But Eugene doesn't hire thugs for their brains."

"Doesn't mean they don't have 'em. Some people consider me a thug, ever consider that?"

I knew she hadn't because sometimes I still caught that gleam of hero worship in her eyes. Now I chalked it up to how good I made her feel rather than any real heroics on my part.

"Okay, fuck. You're right. I can see my car now, which means I'll see your scowling face in about fifteen minutes. Twenty if I don't manage to miss the goats rush hour."

A new farm had opened up on the property to the north and their goats had taken to gathering on the road every day at the same time.

"Good luck."

"Oh crap. I need to pick up wings and thongs first. That's where I was headed when I found the party favors. Make that forty minutes, maybe forty-five."

"Wings and thongs?"

"Wings for dinner, and The Barn Door-branded thongs like we talked about?"

I didn't remember shit about thongs, but maybe that's when she was grinding on my lap and kissing that spot on my neck.

"We'll do it tomorrow. Together."

"I'm already here," she insisted, defiant. "And I'm already headed towards Opey Wings & Things."

Stubborn fucking woman. "I'll meet you there. And if you're not there when I get there, Hennessy, there will be hell to pay."

"I'm willing to risk it."

"I'm not." The more casual she was about all this, the more worried I got. My gut was telling me to worry, and I learned early in my military career to listen to my gut.

"Be there."

"I promise," she sighed with annoyance, but I knew she'd keep her word. Hennessy might fight a little more than I'd like considering who was after her, but she wasn't reckless or stupid.

Still, I moved a little faster, grabbing the key to my bike and heading off the ranch to find my woman. She might not be mine for real, or hell, maybe she was at this point, I didn't even really know. The sex was incredible, the conversation was good, and we hadn't run out of shit to say to each other yet. She cooked like a pro, but none of that added up to mine or any of this being real. Or permanent. Despite all that, keeping her safe *was* on me. That much I knew.

I parked my bike behind the ranch truck I insisted she take just in case McArthur's men were on the lookout for her rental, and walked the half a block to Wings & Things. The place was empty except for two old timers sharing an oversized pizza.

"You guys seen a beautiful redhead?" I asked.

"If I had, I'd be sweet talking her over this pizza instead of this old geezer," one old dude said as he pointed to the other.

"Been a slow day," the kid behind the counter confirmed. "No one but these two for the past couple hours."

TIED

Shit! "Thanks," I said, as that sick feeling in the pit of my stomach turned into a fucking boulder. I stepped back out onto the street, trying to figure out where Hennessy was when she called me. She said she could see the car so that's where I started, beside the old blue truck. To the left was only the municipal building and a long block of no parking signs. Behind me was a park, which meant she was either coming from Main Street or Second Street.

The printer was just off Second Street ,so that was where I headed, hoping like hell she was in there with a defiant grin on her face, while I scowled at her until she apologized for scaring the fuck out of me. I didn't even make it to the printers before I spotted the unopened box of invitations, sitting there mocking me for being too late. They teetered on the edge of the curb, a bad fucking sign if I ever saw one.

I picked them up, jumped on my bike and hurried back to the ranch, calling Hennessy every fifteen seconds the whole way back.

"Hen, it's me. Call me back. Please call me back."

Chapter Twenty-Three

Hennessy

"Thanks Randi, enjoy the rest of your day!"

I couldn't believe spending just an hour walking around this little town while I ran errands was turning me into a person who told people to have a nice day. My old self would have mocked this new version of me, the bitch who smiled for no reason and didn't rush a chatty cashier at the costume shop.

No, I didn't just not rush the older woman, I leaned in and listened keenly as she told me all about the last time someone had rented the black and red angel style wings from her. Who knew this little old town used to have a brothel?

"I will have a nice day, hon, and I can't wait to hear how those wings work out for you. Which one of those hot hunks of heaven is yours?" Randi seemed to know all the guys at the ranch. She rested her chin in her hands and let out a swoony sigh. "They're all yummy though. If only I was a few years younger."

I thought of Slayer's love of older women. "Maybe you're just the right age, Randi."

"Aww. Get outta here," she said with a blushing smile as she waved me out of the store. "Enjoy."

With a final wave, I pushed out of the costume shop and dropped the wings off at the truck Cruz had insisted I take. He was so cute the way he worried about me. I knew it was part of the deal, but part of me couldn't help but feel touched that he cared enough to do it at all.

I knew Eugene's men had been seen around town, but they hadn't made a move, so I figured Homer had told them about the marriage.

"Shit," I said out loud as I reached the truck. I forgot the invitations again, so I headed back towards the printer, hoping I could pick up the invitations before Cruz arrived at Wings & Things. He seriously worried about me, and I didn't want to push his buttons too much.

My errand at the printer took only a few minutes. I tucked the box under my arm and headed down the street again. I stopped at the light and opened the box to peek at the invitations.

"Excuse me miss, where is Montlake Avenue?"

I was too busy admiring the designs to look up at the deep voice. Normally, it would have alarmed me, but this small town living had a way of taking the cynic out of you. Quickly.

"Never heard of it," I said, sliding the box closed. "Sorry."

"That's okay."

That voice sent a shiver of unease through me and turned to the suddenly ominous sounding voice.

"I'm here for you anyway, Hennessy."

A man with thick, curly black hair lunged, and I jumped back, but his arms were longer than I expected, and he caught my wrist.

"No!" I screamed, but nobody heard me.

"Yes," he growled back with a laugh, enjoying the way I struggled with him before he finally yanked me up against his chest. "You've pissed off the boss man."

"Too bad," I said with more confidence than I felt. I tried to take a step back. "He can stay pissed off for all I care."

The man laughed and grabbed me by both arms.

"You're feisty, I like that. A little scrawny for my tastes but a man likes what he likes, I guess."

I kept struggling, even though the guy had at least six inches and eighty pounds on me.

"Don't make this hard on yourself," he hissed.

Then without waiting for a response or asking any of the ten million questions rolling through my mind, he tossed me into the black van at the curb, and I landed on my elbow, which sent a searing pain through all of me.

"Sorry about that," he said.

"Shit man, the old dude's gonna be pissed you hurt her."

That voice sounded younger and unfamiliar, but I didn't bother myself with that side of my dad's life, never wanted any part of it. I only recognized the dark-haired dude because he came to collect me during one of my court-mandated visits with Homer.

"Nah, she's fine. See?" He yanked me up to a sitting position and slid a thick fabric bag over my head, blacking everything out. Then he held my elbow up, yanking it this way and that.

"She'd be screaming a lot louder than that if it was serious. She's tiny. What the fuck was I supposed to do?"

"You're twice her size, you could have just threatened her." The kid had a point, but that type of kindness would probably get him killed in this line of work.

"Where are you taking me?"

My voice sounded muffled through the bag. It was a stupid fucking question. They were taking me to Eugene, I knew that. But I needed more information. At least that's what my heart kept saying. My brain told me to find a way out of this because my heart was stupid, and no one was coming to save me.

"I asked you a question. Where are you taking me?"

"Somewhere nice and quiet where you and boss man can have some alone time."

I didn't need my sense of vision to know he was wearing a suggestive expression. It dropped from every syllable he grunted.

"I'll need to stop and pee if we're leaving Texas."

"Nice try, sugar tits. You can piss when we get where we're going. Or I can just watch. I'm into it if you are."

Ugh, gross. "No thanks." That must mean Eugene was in Texas, which meant he was angrier than I anticipated. Suddenly, I hoped that my heart was right because I wasn't sure there was another way out of this for me.

I don't know how long they drove, at least an hour, maybe more. I lost count somewhere around thirty-one hundred. Eventually the van came to a stop, and I tried to relax my body and slow down my breathing.

But a hand wrapped around my arm, startling the ever-loving fuck out of me. "What the?"

"It's just me, sugar tits. Calm down."

One big calloused hand slid up my thigh, and I kicked out blindly, landing a few glancing blows.

"Settle down, bitch." He shook me, hard, until I stopped fighting. "I won't hurt you, so calm the fuck down. Okay?"

I nodded, but the day I believed a man like that would be my last day breathing. I relaxed when he pulled me from the van. As soon as my feet hit the ground, though, I started running. Blindly. That fucker tied the bag around my neck and trying to get it off slowed me down a lot.

"Dammit," I said as I ran and struggled with the knot at my neck.

I could hear footsteps getting closer, and I tried to run faster and untie the drawstring but, goddammit, it was tangled up.

Suddenly, it felt like a brick wall had caught up to me and pushed me to the ground at fifty miles an hour. I landed with a thud that knocked the wind out of me.

"I guess now we do it the hard way," he said.

He sat on my back and tied my arms behind me, tight enough that my hands started to tingle right away.

"A lot of women would love to be in your position."

I grunted at that.

"Yeah? Then it seems like the logical answer would be to go get one of them, but you guys aren't too keen on logic are you?"

"Smart mouth bitch."

He put a dirty bandana over my mouth and dummy that I was, sucked in a huge breath that knocked me right the fuck out.

Chapter Twenty-Four

Cruz

"Fuck."

Hearing that word on Hardtail Ranch was no surprise, not even when it was a feminine voice saying it. Hearing Peaches say it after a round of finger gymnastics on her computer, was disheartening as fuck.

"Fuckity fuck fuck."

"What?" I couldn't take it anymore. "Just say it, Peaches."

As soon as I realized what happened, I called Gunnar to get Peaches on the job because that's how we did things. We all knew she was a vital fucking part of the Reckless Bastards family, but we all went through Gunnar first out of respect to his status as MC Prez.

"Please."

"Sit," she said, and pointed to the flannel ottoman off to the side. She smiled at her sleeping little boy and the little girl asleep on the sofa beside her.

"And try to keep your volume down." Peaches turned the laptop toward me and tapped a button.

The black screen turned slightly grainy as a color image appeared. Hennessy in her cut-off jeans and gauzy green shirt that made her eyes look the greenest color I had ever seen. She'd just come out of the print shop, a smile on her face as she made her way back to the car, completely oblivious to the man who'd watched her go inside and waited, barely hidden while she chatted with the owner. She was unaware of the man, distracted even when he approached her.

They spoke, and my gut clenched the moment she realized she was in real danger. She took a step back, but it was too late for that. Her fate had been sealed the moment she forgot to scan her surroundings after leaving the print shop.

"Aw, shit, Peaches," I said, even though she couldn't stop what was happening on the screen.

TIED

They verbally went back and forth for a few minutes before Hennessey tried to walk away. The man yanked her back, obviously enjoying having his hands on her a little too much. Then he grabbed her by the arms, lifted her in the air and tossed her into the black van before sliding the door closed. The van took off fast and that's where the clip ended. And began to replay.

"Son of a bitch," I muttered into my fists I held under my chin.

"I know." The sympathy in Peaches' voice nearly undid me, and I didn't need to get emotional right now. Hennessy needed me to be clearheaded, strong. To save her from this old ass mobster.

"We'll find her."

"I know," I huffed at her, unnecessarily, but her tone was pissing me off. "Sorry." I looked down, I still had the box of fucking invitations in my hand.

"It's all right. Look I know you don't want to talk about it, and you'll probably deny it with your last breath, but I know Hennessy is important to you."

She held up her hands defensively when I glared at her. "I'm not saying how or why or when, just that she is. And that means she's important to me."

"That's not necessary, Peaches."

"It is," she said firmly. Her expression dared me to argue with her. I was too distracted and too smart to do that.

"You boys saved my ass more than once. So, if she matters to you, then she matters to me."

I searched for something to say that wasn't over the top sappy or at least a little funny, but nothing came. Thankfully, Peaches saved me from that particular hell.

"I tracked them through town. They drove around for a long time, probably trying to disorient her. But they took a final turn down Route 9."

Shit. "There are no traffic cams, public or private, over there right?"

TIED

Peaches nodded. "Used to be a major transport road for the underworld until about a decade or so ago."

I didn't bother to ask how she knew that, but I was grateful that she did.

"We're blind over there but the fact that they chose that road says that's where they are."

"And that they put some planning into this," Gunnar said from the doorway, a dark frown on his face. "You watch the footage?"

"I did," I said. And there wasn't a snowballs chance in hell that I'd forget the look of fear on her face for a million goddamn years. Worse, it was all my fault. I went against my instincts and all because she batted those fuckin' lashes at me, and I caved. "Fuck!"

Peaches shushed me, and I went outside, needing fresh air as much as wide open space to yell and scream until my head was clear enough to save her.

"We're in this together."

I let out a snort at Gunnar's words. "Are we?"

"Damn right, we are. She's your woman, and we'll go to hell and back to make sure she's safe and back at the ranch."

Nice words, but I didn't really believe them, but I also wasn't stupid enough to turn away help.

"Look, I'm new at being Prez while being a dad. I know, Maisie is mine, and I hate to admit it, but it is different. I *feel* different and yeah, maybe I was hesitant about more trouble."

"Hesitant?"

"Okay, I was a goddamn pussy about it, all right?"

He laughed and I shrugged.

"That sounds about right."

A smile fought to free itself, but I held strong with just a smirk.

"Either way, we're gonna make this McArthur motherfucker sorry he crossed the Reckless Bastards. For real."

I gave one short nod, taking Gunnar at his word. He could be an asshole sometimes, but he was as true blue as they came.

"Okay. What's the plan?"

Gunnar blinked his surprise. "You don't have one?"

"At the moment my plan is to storm Route 9 until we find those fuckers and make them pay, no matter how messy it gets."

Gunnar grinned. "As fun as that sounds, we still have the suicide in the club to think about. Come on, Slayer and Saint are scouting Route 9 as we speak."

That was music to my ears, and I let Gunnar guide me away from the main house and to The Barn Door, where the rest of the MC was ready to have my back, with guns, whiskey, and ganja. As soon as we made a plan and got Hennessy back, two of those would be heading home with me.

With us.

Chapter Twenty-Five

Hennessy

Kidnapped. I can't believe I was fucking kidnapped. And by Eugene McArthur's idiotic henchmen no less. As much as I wanted to be pissed off that this happened, it was fucking inevitable. Not in a *woe is me, my life always goes shitty and takes a left instead of a right*, kind of way.

More in the inevitability of things kind of way. Opey wasn't just a small town, it was one of those idyllic small towns where it was very easy to fall under the easygoing, slow-paced, life is good spell the town weaved around you.

And I had fallen. Hard and fast. Letting my guard down like I was a normal girl with normal parents who would never, ever, in a million years do things like use their daughter in a poker game. Or worse, sell her off to a mobster who had nothing but nefarious plans. This was the price of letting my guard down, of pretending to be normal just for a little while, and I wasn't sure yet, whether or not it had been worth it. If I made it out of this, I'd decide.

It was something to think about later, because right now I pretended I was still knocked out from whatever that shit was on that dirty bandana. It was like a really bad gangster movie. They had my wrists tied together and attached to something just enough above my head to be uncomfortable, but instead of chains hanging from a ceiling, I was attached to a wall. It was cold, and no light crept in under my hood, which meant I was truly fucking…blind.

Footsteps sounded across the room. I stiffened, holding my breath until I could figure something out. The footsteps grew louder and louder until the person stopped in front of me. And unceremoniously tore the hood off me, nearly taking my head with him.

"Good. You're awake." He grunted the words like he didn't mean them.

I recognized the voice right away as the dark-haired man, but it was so bright with enough bare bulbs that it completed the stereotype and bad gangster movie set. It took a moment for my eyes to focus on details, but I knew right away there was someone else with him. I blinked a few more times until a thick crop of dark hair came into view beside a thinner, grayer head of hair.

"Eugene." The word escaped in a gasp before I could stop it.

The old man grinned, and it was the pure definition of villainy.

"Is that happiness I hear, my precious Hennessy?"

"Fuck no," I practically spit the words at him, making him laugh until he coughed.

"Either way, you're mine so it doesn't really matter."

He shook his head and tried to pace, a move that made him look less frightening and less intimidating by the second. He was an old man. Frail and trying hard to hang on to power he only held because of old rules meant to keep old men in power. It was only my compromised position that kept me in full fear mode. He didn't like to be challenged and my running probably made him look like a big fucking idiot.

"Did you really think you could get away from me so easily?"

I had and that was the saddest, maybe the stupidest part of all.

"Hoped is more like it."

"Mouthy cunt!"

His wrinkled old hand, complete with blue veins and liver spots, landed down on my cheek, stinging a little. He was too old and too weak to do any real damage, but I gave a good whimper because his sidekick looked like he might enjoy beating up a woman if given the chance.

"You stupid fucking whore. This could have gone a lot different. I just want you to remember that."

Eugene got right up in my face so that his craggy features and cloudy gray eyes were all I could see. His skin was thin and pale, a sign of his age and frailty. I refused to think about why he had me at such a disadvantage.

Before I could ask what he meant, Eugene took a step back and the rest of the lights in the room flickered to life and revealed a lot more of the room. It looked like a barn or stable, and based on the smell of mildew and decay, it hadn't been active in a long time.

By the far door stood two men, one with a shock of red hair and the other had a black buzzcut. Both of them held machine gun-looking weapons in their hands. Two guys stood in a far corner, armed with two handguns each, holstered at their sides. They stepped aside, and I realized this was all part of the show.

Homer.

My father who was never anything but a good time guy ready with some spare change and my favorite candy bar because it was the only detail he ever remembered about me. And there he was, tied to a metal folding chair. Beaten, bloody, and I couldn't even tell if he was breathing. And apparently, it was all for my benefit.

As if that would move me.

"Wake him up," Eugene barked at the two henchmen guarding my father. They jumped to obey him. One kicked the legs of the chair and the other shook him by the shoulders. Geniuses, really.

"Goddammit!" Eugene marched, slowly, to Homer. He slumped over, still completely out of it. Eugene gave his cheek two firm smacks.

"Ah, there you are Homer. Just in time for the next part!"

Homer's eyelids fluttered open, and he looked around in confusion as his brain worked to put all the pieces together. He focused on Eugene first, and the fear kicked in. Then his gaze landed on me and all the blood drained from his face. "Hennessy?"

"Yeah, it's me." There was no point being angry anymore. I mean, I was furious, but he'd already gotten more than he deserved as far as I was concerned.

"Baby girl." He leaned forward as if he could reach out to me. Instantly, one of the men slammed him back against the chair.

"I'm so sorry." His words were cut off by a half-assed smack from Eugene.

"You're a sorry fucking excuse for a father, that's what you are!" Eugene's voice took on the tone of a much younger man, firm and angry.

"You didn't give me a choice," Homer insisted, staring up at Eugene with something other than fear in his eyes for the first time. Now there was anger there, too.

"We always have a choice, Homer. Your need to win simply overrode your need to protect your daughter, and I took advantage."

He looked so fucking proud of himself it made me sick.

"Neither of you will ever have to worry about winning person of the year award."

They were both two different types of garbage as far as I was concerned. I shook my head, disgusted at both of them and the fact that this is where I ended up, a bad fucking cliché, and it was through no fault of my own. It wasn't because I fell for the wrong man or followed him down the wrong path. Nope, I just got stuck between two warring dumbasses.

Lucky me.

"I'm fine with that." Eugene turned to me with a lecherous look in his eyes, smoothing down his grayish-blue suit as if preparing for a suitor.

"You will stay here until we're married," he said as if that was the end of the discussion. "It could have been a nice ceremony with a beautiful dress and a nice honeymoon, but since we have to do it like this, you'll deal with it."

Ah, there it was. The reason we were all gathered here today. It took me about half a second to decide if I should keep the marriage to myself or let him know. It was clear, Homer hadn't told him, or else he wouldn't be putting on such a show. In the end, my need to let

TIED

this fucker know I had bested him, if only temporarily, won out.

"Oh, didn't you hear? I'm already married. Been a newlywed for about a month now."

Goddamn, it felt good to shit all over his plans like that, but I knew that didn't mean I was free to go. "I would show you the ring but I'm a bit tied up at the moment." Yeah, it felt really fucking good.

For a split second.

The gleam in his cloudy eyes darkened as storm clouds gathered. His lips curled into a semblance of what was supposed to be a smile, but it came off more like a psychotic grimace as he walked towards me until we were face to face once again. His breath smelled of cigar smoke and garlic, and I had to suppress the urge to vomit, knowing that wouldn't go over well with his fragile ego. Gramps was a full blown psycho.

My goal now was to piss him off enough that he didn't do anything stupid, but not so much that he killed me before help arrived. *If* it arrived at all.

"That's really too bad, Hennessy. I would've enjoyed breaking in a young woman with your fire."

His hand cupped my face and then my neck just so the sick bastard could make sure I saw the heat and desire in his eyes.

Eww.

"I guess now I'll have to figure out another way for you and Homer to pay the debt you owe."

He sent me a terrifying look, truly fucking terrifying. I sent a prayer up to anyone who might be listening, to send Cruz and his boys fast and armed.

And definitely before Eugene's creativity kicked in.

I only had a vague idea of the things Eugene and his crime family did, so I had no idea of just how creative he could get and I didn't want to stick around to find out.

Chapter Twenty-Six

Cruz

"Anything yet?"

My question went out to no one in particular. Hell, I didn't even really expect an answer, but asking made me feel like I was doing something to help Hennessy.

"Not since the last time you asked, man. Peaches is upstairs diggin' as fast as she can. Says, if you ask her one more question, she's turning in for the night."

Holden's deep Texas twang had an oddly soothing effect and I nodded, looking around the room at everyone who sat with me. Worried with me.

"Saint and Slayer back yet?"

Gunnar had sent them out to do some recon, to see if we could easily find where McArthur's men would have taken Hennessy. The problem, we learned, was that Route 9 was massive as fuck with at least a dozen different exits that led to at least that many other plots of land. Some were abandoned and some were occupied, but not all were occupied legally, which meant we could be in for a hell of wait.

And that really fucking sucked because it had already been a hell of a wait.

"If they were, Slayer would be in here flirting, eating, and taking all the credit," Gunnar assured me with a weary smile.

"Shit. Sorry." This waiting shit was driving me crazy. It was just like the military all over again, waiting for orders, waiting for instructions or directions, and feeling helpless because I couldn't do shit when it really mattered. "Why am I going so crazy?"

"Sounds to me like you might actually like Hennessy." Aspen sat on the sofa beside Holden, stroking his hair even as she looked at me with a mischievous smirk on her face. "Would that be so terrible?"

"It wouldn't, but that's not what this is. I feel responsible, that's all. I told her I'd take care of her and keep her away from that fucker, and I failed. I fucked up."

"Duh," she said and shook her head. "That's what love is. You want to keep her safe because you vowed to."

"Promised," I corrected her and stood, going to the window in search of even a hint of headlights that would indicate Slayer and Saint were back. With news.

"Tomato, *Tom-ahto*," Aspen shot back with a defiant grin. "You'll figure it out," she sang just as my phone rang.

It was Hennessy.

"Hen. Where are you?" My heart pounded at the silence on the other end of the line. As pissed off as I felt and despite what the evidence said, I hoped Hennessy had just gotten distracted with a sale or something equally minor. Safe. Benign.

"Hen?"

A deep laugh sounded, loud and booming down the line at first. After a few seconds the asshole with the maniacal laugh spoke.

"Wrong. This ain't your precious Hennessy. Nope," he said, letting the 'P' pop dramatically on his lips for emphasis. "She's on her knees getting ready to do exactly what a girl like her is meant to. Her *wifely* duties."

He laughed again, this time putting even more crazy into it, just in case I was operating under the assumption that this asshole was sane.

"Lay one goddamn hand on her, and I will fucking kill you and everyone you hold dear."

He laughed again. "Who? You and your pussy bikers with your matching sashes?"

This time laughter roared out of him. Now I wasn't just pissed off, I was insulted. My hands balled into fists as the fucker kept right on talking and laughing, all the while I listened to any sounds that might help me figure out where he was. More importantly, where Hennessy was.

"You gotta find us first, and you better do it fast before your whore is sold off to some overseas brothel. They love pale ass white women over there."

He left me with those disgusting thoughts and his psychotic laugh before hanging up.

My hand clenched and unclenched in anger while the other had a death grip on the phone, my mind reeling as I stared off into space, picturing Hennessy as she probably was now. Terrified, probably already a little battered if McArthur was the kind of man I thought he was.

I could only hope that Hennessy fought just enough to keep herself alive before we found her, because I knew for damn sure that we would. We had to. I couldn't bear the thought of losing another person I could have saved. *Should* have fucking saved.

A soft feminine hand slid along the length of my forearm, gently extricating the phone from my grip. I looked up quickly, heart pounding with the unrealistic hope that it was Hennessy's touch. It wasn't, of course, it was Peaches.

"I think you kept him on the line long enough if that's any consolation," she said with an uneasy smile.

"This is her phone, right?"

I nodded, but Peaches was already on the floor in the middle of the living room with her legs crossed and covered by a laptop, my phone in her hands with a plug coming out of its ass.

"Perfect. We can find her phone. I put the app on when we went out to lunch a few weeks ago."

Peaches flashed a smile at her own genius, and I made a note to get her something expensive and geeky as fuck for helping me save Hennessy.

"Of course you did. I'm just glad you're on our side."

"Lucky thing I am with the trouble you guys always seem to find." Her lips twitched at the irony of her statement. "Good thing for us that you guys are all heroes."

I barked out a bitter laugh at that, not feeling all that heroic at the moment. "I think you mean we all have a hero complex."

Peaches shrugged. "All that matters is that you're there when someone needs you. Like now," she said and turned her attention back to the screen in front of her.

"Here, drink this." Holden held a short glass half-full with amber liquid in front of my face.

"What is it?"

"White Zinfandel, what the fuck do you think it is?" The glass remained where it was, waiting for me to take it. "Whiskey."

I took the glass and knocked it back in one short, calming, fire-inducing shot. "Thanks."

"No problem. We'll find her." Holden's stoic certainty was comforting, but I also knew it was likely bullshit, just as he knew. That was the shit part about war. There were always people who didn't make it back. There was always collateral damage.

"I know," I said. I knew we'd find her. Because I would scour every fucking inch of Opey and beyond until I found her.

"I'm just worried about what shape she'll be in when we finally get to her."

I couldn't fucking stand the thought of that asshole ruining Hennessy, taking away her ability to live a normal healthy life. I didn't want her to become a victim of a different kind of war.

"You care about her."

His words came out easily, not a question and not an accusation. There was a bit of surprised amusement, but I let it go since he was trying to help.

"We'll get her back here and give you another chance to screw things up," he said and clapped me on the back twice as hard as he needed to.

I smiled up at him and flipped him the bird. "You always say the sweetest things to me, Holden."

But secretly, I hoped he was right. I hoped when we found Hennessy, she was okay, that nothing more than a day of rest and pampering could cure. Then maybe, just maybe, I might get a chance to figure out why the fuck my heart was beating out of my chest. Why I felt the need to fuck some shit up.

Holden barked out another laugh and clapped me on the back before he refilled my glass to the halfway mark. "Same thing Aspen always says to me, except it sounds much sexier when she says it."

"I'll be sure to tell her you said so," I deadpanned.

"Asshole," he grinned and took the glass from my hands, setting it on the nearest table. "Come one, I know just what will get your mind off things."

"Yeah?" Because I would love to hear what fucking magic porno trick would accomplish that feat in the moment.

"Yeah. We're going to the armory to pick out what we're gonna use on these assholes when we find 'em."

I stopped and smiled because it was the only damn thing that stood a chance in hell of cheering me up. "Let's do it."

Chapter Twenty-Seven

Hennessy

"Hennessy, you have to believe me, baby girl. I never planned for any of this to happen." Homer sat bent over his chair, face bruised and bloody, with guilty eyes on me.

I wished I could have sympathy for the pitiful figure he made, slumped over a chair as all of his bad decisions finally came down on him. And me.

"Yeah? What exactly did you mean when you added *me* to the pot in the first damn place?"

He let out another one of those sorry-ass sighs, the one that had me and Mom forgiving him every time he gambled away the rent money or stole the few dollars set aside for my field trip fees. Always, we forgave him.

"The hand was mine."

"Except it wasn't. You can't ever be sure until the cards are flipped over or was another bullshit lesson?"

He'd taught me all about poker, every variety from Texas Hold 'em to draw and stud, even Omaha. I knew them all.

"I know you're angry at me. But I truly am sorry, baby girl."

"I know, Homer." I knew he was sorry, now that the proverbial chickens had come home to roost. Right now I had bigger issues, like the crazy old man who had some dark plans for me, and the biker who might or might not come to my rescue. "I know."

He nodded and turned away just as the only door I could see opened and Eugene walked inside, his favorite henchman at his side.

"Hennessy. I hope you've had some time to think about your attitude. I haven't decided what to do with you, yet, but several options are on the table."

An unconscious shiver stole through me at his words, because I didn't need to be the *Law & Order* expert that I was to know I wouldn't appreciate any of those options. Never mind the fact that I didn't believe Eugene at all. The man was a gangster, a criminal and worse, he was a goddamn snake.

"I think I've been pretty fucking calm since I was *kidnapped*."

He let out a low chuckle at first that gained steam as he carried on laughing like he was auditioning to be a villain in a comic book movie.

"You've got spunk, I'll give you that. Stupid, but you've got spunk."

The henchman stayed behind Eugene as he made his way over to Homer first, turning and yanking his chair until it faced me.

"I guess you inherited your stupid from this one."

"I'm not the one who accepted a bet from someone who couldn't pay it back." It wasn't smart to taunt him, but at this point, did I really have anything to lose?

"Maybe not," he said with a sneer. "But all that matters is that I have you right where I want you."

I felt, more than saw, the moment his intent changed. It went from dark and angry to dark and something else, something that made me shiver with disgust. Fear? Evil?

Eugene grew bored quickly with Homer and ambled toward me, his angry-looking muscle man looming behind him menacingly.

"Nothing to say to that?"

Not really. "You have me where you want me. For now."

The old fucker better enjoy it while he could, because as soon as I was free I'd beat the holy fuck out of him until he was dead.

He let out a rusty old laugh and kept walking until he was close enough to block the chill that puckered my nipples through my t-shirt and covered my skin in goosebumps. Eugene's gaze settled on my nipples, and he licked his lips as one hand went to my thigh, stroking slowly.

"You make an excellent point. I might as well enjoy you while I can."

His hand was slow and shaky as it slid up my thigh, stopping when a knobby knuckle brushed against my pussy.

Thankfully, the thick denim seam dulled his touch. "Don't touch me!"

Eugene only laughed harder, like it was all some big damn joke.

"Oh, I'll touch you as much as I like. You *are* mine after all."

"No. I'm. Not."

It was useless to struggle but I couldn't help it, my body wouldn't let me do anything but fight against his touch, against his bad intent for me.

"Not yet," he snarled angrily and let his hand slide up past my pussy, up over my hips to cup my waist.

"But goddamn, my cock aches to slide into that tight young pussy of yours."

Eugene's words were punctuated by the clumsy way he squeezed my tits, like they were stress balls.

"And fuck me, these tits. Tight and perky, just how a nice pair of tits should be."

I closed my eyes tight against his assault, continuing to jerk and squirm away from his touch that made me want to puke. I kept moving around, making it hard for him to cop a feel, but the old fucker was determined, squeezing my tits like chew toys and pinching my nipples with a nasty old man groan.

"Oh fuck!" His hand flew across the right side of my face. "I had big fucking plans for you Hennessy! I would have given you the world for the price of entry into that sweet cunt of yours."

Shit! Okay, so the old man did have enough fire to get a good slap going because, holy fuck that hurt.

"Fucker!" I blurted out.

"Exactly!" Eugene stepped closer and put his hands on my waist before he leaned in and pulled my nipple with his mouth, sucking it wet through the fabric of my t-shirt.

Oh my God. I wanted to puke.

"No! Stop!" I squirmed and twisted at my waist, flailing my legs in every direction until the perverted old fucker had no choice but to step back.

"I. Said. No."

He threw his head back and laughed. The sound was raw and goddamn terrifying.

"It really is too bad you decided to run. We could have had a lot of fun together."

If I didn't mind banging a decrepit old mobster for the rest of my life, which didn't sound all that fun.

"It's really too bad you can't get a woman the old fashioned way."

Anger flashed, and he stepped forward. "The old fashioned way? That's what you want?"

I didn't say anything. I couldn't as fear struck me cold at the look in his eyes. Eugene leaned in and pulled out a knife that he slid under the hem of my t-shirt, letting the cool metal touch my skin every now and again just because he could. When he reached the neckline, the knife cut through the t-shirt like butter and it hung open, showing off my red and white bra.

"Whoring yourself up for your new husband?"

I nodded with a smile. "He has *no* problem getting me all hot, wet, and ready."

The knife slipped under the bra and sliced through the fabric easily, revealing my tits to every set of eyeballs in the room. Including my father's.

"Now boys, ain't that a fine set of titties?"

Agreement went up all around, and if I gave a damn about it, I might have felt flattered instead of repulsed.

"Great, now all my dreams have come true."

TIED

"Shut your fucking mouth before I let all my boys have a go at you. Would your precious man still want you after that?"

Probably not, but I kept my mouth shut because the old man was serious now.

"That's what I thought." He tugged at the snap on my jeans until it gave and tugged on my zipper, a move that didn't require a fucking psychic to know what was coming next.

His henchman stood a few feet back, but his gaze never left my tits, and it was impossible to ignore the boner he sported. Or the machine gun draped across one shoulder. When he licked his lips I turned away, but it was the wrong fucking way because my gaze landed on Homer who looked tortured and ashamed, more emotional than I had ever seen him.

The agony on his face served as the perfect distraction when Eugene's old wrinkled fingers slipped between my panties and my pussy, his crusty old fingertips dangerously close to my clit.

"No!" The word came out automatically, as if even my body was disgusted by this piece of shit.

"Oh come on now, Hennessy. You already gave it up to that filthy fucking biker. Now you're too good for me?"

His words were angry and his jerky movements matched, two fingers plunged deep into my pussy without regard for my own readiness.

My legs kicked out, and one hit the old man and sent him staggering back and right into the arms of his henchman.

"I said no, you rapist piece of dog shit!"

The henchman jumped between us as if I could go anywhere with my arms handcuffed to a fucking wall.

"You okay, Boss?"

"Help me up," Eugene shouted angrily, looking around to make sure none of his men saw that moment of weakness, or worse, thought to exploit it at the wrong moment.

TIED

"Get this bitch down on her knees where she fucking belongs!"

Oh, he was good and pissed off now, and I was in trouble.

Reality had set in, fast and cold, and tears silently streamed down my cheeks. The henchman ignored my emotions as he loosened one side of the cuffs and unlatched me from the wall.

"If you try to run, I'll shoot you. If you hurt the boss, I will shoot you."

"Might as well fucking shoot me now and get it over with." Because if that old fuck thought I would put his wrinkly old cock in my mouth, his brain was worse off than I thought.

He laughed. "Tempting, but not until the time is right." One meaty hand landed on my shoulder and shoved me down until I was on my knees.

"Here you go, Boss."

Eugene waved him off and stood, looming over me like the shadow of a man he was, a dark smile lighting up his face.

"Since you want to act like a stupid, worthless whore, that's how I'll treat you."

He reached forward and grabbed a handful of my hair.

"Go on and do what whores do. Suck it!"

His hips jerked forward while his flaccid cock waved around my face, silver hairs brittle and bent in all directions threatening to poke out an eye. Maybe two.

I did my best to keep my mouth shut, a difficult task for a mouthy chick like me, but desperate times and all that. Left and then right, I jerked my head even as Eugene pulled harder and harder.

One hand landed across my cheek again. "Open your fucking mouth."

TIED

I shook my head in defiance, knowing this was a dangerous game but also knowing I couldn't give in. Not now. Not on this.

"All right then. Let's do it your way." He produced a handgun and pressed it to the middle of my forehead. "I said, open the fuck up. And I better not feel any fucking teeth."

Knowing I was beat, I did what he said, ignoring the evil smile on his face.

Chapter Twenty-Eight

Cruz

"We can count on this fucker having a lot of men," Gunnar was saying when Holden and I returned from the armory with two trucks loaded up with all the fire power we could possibly need.

"Peaches, tell the guys what you found."

Peaches didn't bother to stand, smiling as she rocked Stone to sleep in her arms.

"McArthur isn't some rinky-dink crime boss. That's the bad news. He's the head of the second largest Irish crime family on the east coast."

"Last I checked, this wasn't the fucking east coast," Slayer added with a bite to his words. "If he's so badass, why are they using a fucking broke down warehouse to keep her? A motel would be less conspicuous."

Gunnar nodded and turned his attention to Saint.

"What else did you find?"

"At least a dozen men on the outside, protecting the building and the perimeter. My guess is there are at least double that amount on the inside. The place is big as fuck, though."

Saint raked a hand through his dark hair and blew out a breath. "Who the fuck knows where they're holding her."

His gaze looked around the room and I knew exactly what he saw. Not enough fucking men to go head to head with Eugene McArthur.

"We sure this is where Hennessy is?" Holden's deep voice asked the question none of the rest of us had the balls to ask.

"Yeah, are we sure? I can't go in there, guns blazing and find it's the wrong fucking place."

The idea of it made me sick to my fucking stomach, storming the property and finding Hennessy wasn't there, or worse, was already gone. Shipped off to parts unknown.

TIED

"I can give you the only certainty I can," Peaches said and handed my phone to Slayer who handed it to me. "Call her."

I stared at the phone like it was a bomb, but I knew it had to be done. I dialed, grinning when the same asshole picked up the phone.

"Better hurry up asshole, your whore is about to drown in some jizz when my boys finish running this train on her." He laughed again and hung up.

"That motherfucker is dead!"

Gunnar smacked the kitchen table and stood. "All right everyone, get your shit together. We're out of here in five."

I frowned. "Five? You said stealth was how we should do this."

"Yeah, that was before these fuckers threatened to rape your woman. Come on. Everybody and that means you too, Ford."

Rape. The word bounced around in my head until fire pumped through my veins. White hot fire that fueled an even hotter rage that burned my insides, my flesh, and my hair as I stared out the window on Route 9, watching the Texas sky at night fly by. McArthur and his men could have put Hennessy through any number of horrors, I just hoped she could fucking recover from them.

This was some heavy shit for a woman to go through.

We parked across the street from the old property, hiding our bikes and trucks among the overgrown brush and the tall trees that needed some maintenance. It took us a few minutes before we got our shit together, sending Ford and Slayer to double check the numbers. I should have been right up there in the front with my brothers, but I was too close. Too fucking emotional to do anything but bash some heads and go get my woman.

"Nine down on the perimeter," Slayer mumbled into the comms. "Three unaccounted for."

"One," Saint corrected, out of breath. "Come in on the west side of the building, away from the freeway."

TIED

In just over a minute we all gathered at the nearest entry point where Slayer and Saint waited for us. Ford was on backup with orders to shoot anyone not a member of the Reckless Bastards, or Hennessy.

"Breach in sixty," Gunnar said and sent Saint, Holden and Wheeler around to the other exit point while me, him and Slayer got into position.

Fifty-five seconds later the lights went out. Five seconds later, we stormed inside the dark building and broke it up in a grid pattern, clearing every room of any live obstacles before we moved on.

"Gunnar, down!" He ducked without clarification and it saved his life as I put two bullets into a blond with an Uzi.

"Thanks, man."

"Clear!" Slayer was several rooms ahead, and I hurried to catch up, eager to find Hennessy. My heart thundered behind my chest as everything moved at half-speed.

"Listen to that."

I closed my eyes and listened. It was the sound of chaos which meant McArthur's men knew we were here.

"We have to hurry."

Gunnar nodded and took off first. "I'll cover you both. Go now!"

We cleared another long hall as gunfire sounded on the other side of the building. Long-ago forgotten backup generators provided extra light in corners as we drew closer to the shouts. No, the screams.

A woman's screams.

"Hennessy!"

I took off at a dead sprint, my only focus getting to Hennessy and making the fucking scream top.

"Hennessy, I'm coming!"

"Stop!"

Gunnar's voice was proof that no solider every really forgot their training. My feet stopped, and I turned to him, pissed off but waiting with barely restrained patience.

"You go through that door without backup and you're dead. How's that gonna help your girl?"

Slayer clapped me on the shoulder. "We got your back. I'll go in first and lay down cover fire while I search for Hennessy. You come in next and find her. Gunnar will cover you. Right?"

Gunnar nodded his agreement. "On your count, Slayer."

The next few seconds unraveled in slow motion as Slayer kicked in the door and put five bullets inside the two men guarding the door. I moved in next, shooting moving men while I scanned the large cavernous room for Hennessy.

"No!" Her scream sounded near the back, and I crouched low and made my way to her, picking off whoever tried to stand in my way.

"Hennessy!"

She was screaming and crying as if her life was in danger, and when I got closer, I could see why. That old fucker, Eugene fucking McArthur had Hennessy, *my* fucking Hennessy, with her tits bared for all to see, his hands and mouth having a good time with her tits.

In three steps, I was at Hennessy's side with one hand wrapped around that motherfucker's throat and a gun aimed at his forehead.

"Shoot this motherfucker!" He cried out. His frail body shook with indignation and he continued to shout his outrage into the room.

"Not so fun when you don't have your thugs at your side, is it?"

I whispered the words in his ear just to make sure that fucker knew how close I was to him.

"You're a dead man," he whined.

"Wrong answer." I cracked him in the head with the butt of the gun until he went down to his knees.

"You all right, Hen?"

She nodded, breathless, as a smile tried to form on her lips. "Uhm…" Her words turned to tears, and Hennessy buried her head in her hands.

McArthur laughed, and I lost it, forgetting about Hennessy completely as I let my fists fly into his face, his body. Pretty much anywhere guaranteed to cause him as much pain as humanly possible before I shot the motherfucker.

Chapter Twenty-Nine

Hennessy

Never in my entire life had I ever been so happy to see another human being. At least not that I could remember. But what would remain forever etched into my memory was the sight of Cruz stalking toward me with murderous rage in his black eyes, big hands flexing in preparation to do maximum damage. As much as I hated that he had to see me like this, being treated like trash with my body exposed for all to see, my body, my heart, and even my brain rejoiced at the sight of him.

My body continued to rage against Eugene's touch, his cold, paper-thin skin, his thin, chapped lips against my nipple. I wasn't sure enough hot water existed to make me clean again, but still my body fought against his assault.

I heard my name but my eyes slammed shut against his touch, at least until I felt him let go of my nipple. Cruz held Eugene by the throat with one hand, glaring at him hard enough to stop the old fuck's heart. His breathing was ragged, his eyes full of black rage, and he produced a gun and aimed it at Eugene's head, whispering something in his ear that made Eugene crazed with anger.

There was so much gunfire, so many flashes of light that I couldn't hear anything. I could barely see what was happening right in front of me, but I watched, nearly transfixed or maybe it was shock, by the sight of Cruz pounding his fists into Eugene's face.

I should have felt horrified to see him beating the shit out of an old man, but the old dude had it coming, and to be honest, seeing Cruz's reaction to what he'd seen meant he cared. It meant I mattered to him, and for some reason *that* mattered to me.

"Ready to get the fuck outta here?"

Gunnar didn't wait for an answer, leaning over my cuffs. "We'll get those off as soon as we can. You good?"

TIED

I gave a sharp nod, glancing just past Gunnar to Cruz still raining his fists down on Eugene. The sorry old dude barely put up a fight.

"I can make it out of here," I said to Gunnar. My gaze went to Cruz once again.

Gunnar's lips twisted into a smirk. "Cruz will be fine. We'll make sure of it."

I gave another nod. "Okay. Let's go, wait…where's Homer?"

"Homer?"

"My dad. The reason I'm in this mess," I shouted over the gunfire.

"There!" Homer was completely out of it, which left a knot of worry in my gut because, apparently, I still gave a shit about him. He was my dad ,and that seemed harder to shake than a nicotine habit.

Gunnar pushed me behind him and turned to Slayer.

"Grab that old man."

I couldn't see Slayer's response because Gunnar's massive frame shielded me from everything. When he turned those big steely blue eyes on me, I had to resist the urge to take a step back. He was intimidating as fuck, but Gunnar was no threat. His gaze raked over my body, and suddenly I wasn't so sure. Then he yanked his t-shirt over his head and tugged it over my nakedness.

"There. Come on." He pulled me a foot and stopped again. "Don't take your hand off me," he said as he put one of my hands on his belt, "and stay by my side unless I tell you to run."

I nodded even as Gunnar turned and started to walk, certain I'd follow his orders.

I try to look around, but it wasn't just Gunnar's massive back that blocked my view. It was the darkness the whole place had been plunged in a few minutes ago, lit up rapidly by the nonstop gunfire going off all around me. I couldn't walk with my eyes closed, so I couldn't help but notice the dead bodies and lifeless eyes, the blood everywhere, permeating the air with a coppery scent that did not mix well with gunpowder.

The door was just a few feet away, the path clear now that Gunnar had put three shots into the armed man with the automatic weapon aimed at us. I chanced a look back at Cruz, still pounding Eugene even as someone tried to pull him off. They fought, Cruz and another man I didn't recognize. Another man joined in, punching him in the back.

I yelled, "Cruz!"

Gunnar yanked me forward. "Cruz will be fine," he barked and dragged me the last few feet out of the stuffy building and out into the fresh Texas night air.

"Get Cruz the fuck outta there," he yelled at someone, though there was no one around us, and I was too exhausted, too terrified to ask more.

"Slow down your breathing so you don't hyperventilate." He breathed in and out until I followed along, keeping each breath slow and steady.

"Good."

My breathing was starting to get back to something resembling normal when another wave of gunfire erupted inside the building, which from the outside, looked like some kind of warehouse or factory. At least seven, maybe eight gunshots rang out, echoing on the silent night and inside the mostly empty building.

Immediately, my eyes went to my surroundings, doing a mental head count, even though I already knew who *wasn't* here yet. Gunnar was by my side, his scowl going to each of his men. Saint and Holden came around one side of the building, guns in hand and gazes never still.

Wheeler appeared next, a cut marring his handsome face, but he didn't seem to notice as his gaze went to Gunnar, silently communicating something I didn't understand. Next, Slayer strutted out, hair blowing in the wind thanks to his lazy long-legged gait, wide eyes and a slightly crazed smile that said he flourished in times like these.

A moment later I noticed something, or rather *someone* else at Slayer's side. Homer. He was barely hanging on to the man in his nearly unconscious state and the truth was, Slayer carried him out.

"Shit," I muttered. As much as I hated the man, I didn't want to see him like that. I tried to stand, to go to him even though there was fuck all I could do to help, but my legs wouldn't work. "Fuck."

"Stay here," Gunnar barked, his voice firm but not menacing. I might have been offended if my body was cooperating and movement was possible.

I sat where I was, legs bent so my knees rested under my chin, Gunnar's t-shirt covering every bare inch of flesh aside from my face and arms, gazed fixed on the only door I could see. Waiting for Cruz to appear.

Any moment he would appear.

He had to.

I waited what felt like an eternity for Cruz to come out, willing him to appear in the door. On his hands or he knees, I didn't give a shit as long as he was there. Alive. Flashing that cocky smile. Somehow, I managed to make it to my feet, but pacing was out of the question so I wrapped my arms around myself.

"Come on, Cruz. Come out." He had to be all right. Nothing would be okay ever again if he wasn't all right. I couldn't let Cruz get hurt—or worse—fighting a battle that wasn't even his.

Or mine.

"Sure took your sweet ass fuckin' time, didn't ya?"

Slayer's good natured words sent a lightning rod of ice down my spine, and I blinked twice to focus my vision, blurred with tears before my brain registered what I was seeing. *Who* I was seeing, to be more specific.

"Cruz!" My legs wobbled on my way to him, but I was determined to push through the pain and the fatigue, until my arms were wrapped around his narrow waist.

"You're okay. Fuck, you're okay."

His deep chuckle sounded through thick, heaving exhales. "You worried about me, wifey?"

Wifey. Not gonna lie, that shit sounded really good in the moment.

"Of course I was. You're my ride home."

At those words, Cruz wrapped his thick arm around me, nearly suffocating me with his bicep, and squeezed. I don't know how long we stood like that, with our arms wrapped around each other, just lost in feeling one another. His heart raced against my chest and his face nestled in the crook of my neck.

"Fuck, I'm glad you're all right," he said. Cruz pulled back and studied my face, a black wave of anger flashed at the sight of me in Gunnar's t-shirt. "You *are* all right, aren't you?"

"Better now, thanks to you." I didn't want to talk about what did or didn't happen inside the walls of that building. Hell, I didn't even want to think about it. Not ever but especially not right now.

"Can we get the hell outta here?"

The corners of his mouth tipped into a lazy smile, and Cruz nodded, pressing a kiss to my forehead. "Abso-fucking-lutely, babe."

With a growl he leaned forward and pulled me close with one of those dark, charming smiles that said he was about to lead me to hell, and my only concern was the road trip playlist. Then his lips were on mine, a slow gentle kiss that ignited a fire deep in my belly. It spread out in slow waves that got bigger and bigger with every passing moment.

I clung to his wide shoulders and let him in, savoring the way I felt with his thick arms wrapped around my waist, his erotic growl sending a shiver through my whole body.

"About that getting the hell out of here thing..."

Cruz laughed and flung a lazy arm around my shoulder as he guided me toward a truck near the road. I tried hard to ignore how well we fit together, in and out of bed. We fit a hell of a lot better than two people only conveniently married.

TIED

An exhausted sigh flew from my lips as Cruz helped me into the pickup truck, and I closed my eyes and relaxed against the headrest, as much as I could relax without closing my eyes. If I closed my eyes all I saw was Eugene.

If I kept them open, all I saw was Cruz.

Chapter Thirty

Cruz

"How's she holding up, Crus?"

I wasn't at all surprised to open my front door and find Peaches standing there with a heavy bag in each hand, a sympathetic smile on her face.

I shrugged and stepped back, taking one of the bags from her. "Been in the shower for about ten minutes. Figured she needed a minute or two to reset. Wash off." To get that old fucker's touch off her gorgeous delicate skin. "She'll be fine."

"Trying to convince me or yourself?"

"Yes," I answered honestly and robotically removed the massive amount of food from the first bag. "Holy shit, for real?"

She shrugged. "You know how Martha gets when she's worried. Besides, it might be a few days before she's feeling like herself." The look in her eyes told me

Gunnar had shared how we found Hennessy. A sight I wish I could bleach from my fucking memory.

"Right. Thanks Peaches." I was too fucking tired to think about things like cooking meals right now. I was worried as hell about Hennessy and I didn't know how to ask her if she was all right. If I needed to go back and make sure none of the McArthur clan ever took another breath. But I couldn't. Could I? Did I even have the right to ask those questions when she was my wife in name only?

And did that mean she would want a divorce or annulment now that Eugene McArthur was nothing but a memory?

"Wow, that was intense to watch. Wanna talk about it?"

Fuck yes. "Nope. I'm good."

"Liar." Peaches flashed a smile and shook her head. "Go slow and don't be afraid to ask her what she needs."

"Thanks for the advice." My tone was sarcastic but I was grateful for the words. "Anything else?"

"Feed her. Food and sex are the perfect distraction for just about anything, Cruz. Remember that." She wrapped one arm around me and pressed her big red lips to my cheek in a loud, smacking kiss. "Good night."

"Night." Peaches' words stayed with me long after she was gone and the sounds of the upstairs shower was the only other sound in the cabin while I laid out all the food, unsure what Hen might feel like eating tonight. If anything. If food and sex were the perfect distraction, we had enough food to last at least a week.

And enough desire to get us through the next year, at least. *Go slow*, echoed in my mind as I climbed the stairs, an idea forming the closer I got to the master bedroom and more importantly, the master bath. A gentle push and the door opened, revealing a thick cloud of steam that made it impossible to see even a foot in front of me. "Hen?"

She gasped. "Cruz?"

"It's me. You okay in here?"

"Mmhmm." Her words were muffled, almost like she was trying to hold back tears, which tore my fucking heart out.

I slid the door open and found those big green eyes staring up at me, red and slightly puffy.

"Oh, Hennessy." Without regard to the fact that I'd already showered and washed McArthur's blood off me, I stepped inside the hot spray and wrapped Hennessy in my arms.

I ignored the feel of her curves as she cried her eyes out. She cried big, bawling sobs that made her soul quake and small, whimpering cries that had the power to kill me. I held her while she expelled her demons from the night. I held her tight, wishing I could have done more to slay this particular demon for her, wishing I could have gotten there sooner.

"Cruz. Thank you."

No other words could have sent that shaky breath rushing out of my chest. "I'm sorry I didn't get there sooner."

"I knew you'd come." Her small hand cupped my face on one side as her thumb traced the line of my jaw. "I'm so fucking glad you did."

"I would kill him all over again for you if I could, Hen." Those tears threatened to fuck me up, bad, and I had to make them stop. "What can I do?"

"Make me forget him, Cruz. Erase him from my mind. Please. I just want to forget."

That was all I needed to hear before I swooped in and claimed her lips, taking my time to savor the plump deliciousness of Hennessy's mouth. She was pliant and receptive, eager to get lost in the pleasure those kisses promised. She wanted to forget, and I was happy to give her something else to remember.

On and on the kiss went until my cock was rock hard even behind my wet clothes, I was too close to losing my shit. This was about making *her* forget, not just getting my dick wet.

"Hen," I moaned and pressed a kiss to her forehead. Her jaw. Her right shoulder and then her left. Her collarbone.

"Cruz, please."

I smiled and stepped from the shower, taking her with me and wrapping a towel around her body so I could take my time drying off every inch of her until she trembled with need.

"I think you might still be wet right here," I told her and brushed the soft fabric across a beaded nipple.

"Not just there," she moaned. She was into it, but she was still thinking about *him*.

"Good to know." I let the towel drop to the floor and took a step back to rid myself of my wet clothes until I was naked with my cock straining out to reach her. "Come here."

I was greedy for her and as soon as Hennessy was close enough, I pulled her into my arms and lifted her in the air until those thick thighs wrapped around my body. Our lips found each other instantly, frantic in our need to come together, both of us in a heightened emotional state that, when combined with arousal, threatened to be combustible.

We made it into the bedroom and as reluctant as I was to take my lips from hers, I did, tossing her onto the bed so I could watch her titties jiggle. Those strawberry-tipped nipples were hard as a rock and my mouth watered.

"You're too far away," she said, her soft voice reminding me of my duty tonight. Operation Distraction was all about Hennessy and it started at those perfectly plump pink lips.

"Is this better?" Our bodies were pressed up against each other, the weight of mine pressing her deeper into the mattress, our breaths mingled in the wisp of a breath that separated us. Before Hennessy could answer, I was devouring her mouth again. Hot and wet and needy, she opened up to me and gave me everything she had in that kiss, and greedy bastard that I was, I took it.

I took it all.

"Better," she moaned.

But we could do better than better. With a goal in mind, my mouth left hers, and I dragged my lips across soft porcelain skin, kissing her jaw and down the long, feminine column of her neck. My lips skidded across her collarbone, pausing so my tongue could slip into the pulsing dip at the base of her throat and moving on. "Hen."

"Yes," she moaned, turned on and breathless. Now she was distracted.

My mouth covered the landscape of her body, lingering for a long time on her gorgeous tits, big and meaty with tips so suckable she almost came from the love I lavished on them. I kissed down the curve of her waist until it flared out to her hips, licking a trail of heat over her hipbone, and I headed across her belly to the other one. I couldn't cross without stopping to pay some attention to her belly button, enjoying the shocked gasp she let out at the touch of my tongue. "Still with me, Hen?"

"Still. Here."

"Excellent." Not one inch of her incredible curves escaped my mouth, not even those shapely legs. The sexy groan she let out when I sucked the skin at the back of her knee nearly made me come, but this was about her. All about her.

"Cruz, please," she begged when I turned her onto her belly and started kissing her at the bottom of her hair line, making my way down one shoulder and then the next, down the gentle slope of her spine and that sexy little dip at the top of her round ass. And just as I made way down to her thighs, Hennessy arched her back and sent me face to face with swollen pink lips, shiny with need. "Fuck, yes!"

I palmed those sweet ass cheeks and held her exactly where I wanted her, watching the way her pussy pulsed with need, following the path of one single drop as it slid down her thigh, before leaning forward to lap it up.

"Fuck!"

I smiled and let out a small puff of air that sent a shiver through her before I buried my face in her pussy, licking and sucking her until the only man she remembered was me. Until the only hands she dreamed about touching her were these hands, this finger as it slid deep inside her asshole.

"Oh fuck, Cruz!" She was wild, crazed with desire as her head thrashed back and forth. I wished I could enjoy the view but I was too busy lapping up all the sweet honey that dripped from her cunt, slurping her juices until she cried out. "Cruz!"

Fuck yeah, just what I wanted to hear, my name falling from her lips because she couldn't contain her pleasure. Couldn't stand the onslaught of ecstasy. When Hennessy reached around and grabbed a fistful of hair, pressing my face into her pussy, I gave her what she wanted. She took control of the moment, and I let her, licking and sucking every inch of her pussy I could get my mouth on. I moaned and she fell to the bed.

"Cruz, yes!"

"Fuck, I love the way you say my name when you're all fuckin' hot and need to come."

She squeaked out a laugh when I flipped her over, never giving her a moment to catch her breath before my mouth was on her again. Holding her thighs open so I could see every move she made and watch every drop of desire that fell from her pussy, I licked her from bottom to top, taking in the way her eyes crinkled at the corners before falling shut, the way her head fell back and her mouth opened to let some of the pleasure escape.

Her body shook. It quivered and vibrated and I never let up, flicking my tongue against her clit until she wrapped her legs around my neck, making breathing impossible but I didn't give a fuck. I breathed in the scent of her pussy as it leaked, shoving my tongue deep inside her pussy as she fucked my mouth.

"Cruz. Oh God Cruz, yes! Oh fuck!"

She was close. I could feel the way she tightened around my tongue, and I didn't change anything. Her hips moved faster and faster, her hand gripped my hair hard enough to bring tears to my eyes and my tongue moved like it was powered by the energizer bunny, licking and sucking and lapping at her until she exploded. I moaned against her and that only intensified her orgasm as my cock began to leak.

"Cruz," she cried for me to stop even as her hand continued to grip my hair and even as she continued to rub her slick cunt all over my face.

"Oh, Cruz. Please."

Not *please stop*, just please. I gave her what she wanted, getting lost in the pleasure of driving her out of her mind when another orgasm tore through her. It was short and fast, like the beautiful blast of a supernova, her body suspended in the most erotic arch I'd ever seen, nipples pointing towards the sky, back bowed so she couldn't get away from my tongue if she tried.

"Cruz," she said minutes later, her voice a warning as another orgasm worked its way from her body. Her pussy pulsed, slower and harder now, and I knew what was coming and curled a tongue around her clit, sucking hard until a flood of moisture rushed out of her body, and she went slack in my arms.

Now that motherfucker was forgotten.

Chapter Thirty-One

Hennessy

It was fucking weird the way life worked out sometimes. Just when I thought things couldn't get any worse, I got kidnapped and assaulted by a mobster. Just when I'd lost hope in humanity, a group of badass bikers swooped in to rescue me like Prince Charming's older, hotter, bad boy brothers.

It was also weird how I started to develop feelings for my husband of convenience. My step-brother actually. I couldn't help it, not after the way he held me and loved me so gently last night. No one had ever made me feel as precious and as important as Cruz had throughout the night. I'd asked him to make me forget, and he'd taken it a step further and given me a night I could never, ever forget.

"Penny for your thoughts?" Peaches walked beside me, and I was grateful she hadn't pushed me to talk.

"That's about what they're worth, to be honest." My thoughts were all over the place, starting with what happened next. Was Cruz expecting me to leave and send him a quickie divorce in the mail? Had anything changed for him? Was Homer already saddled up to someone else's gambling table?

"How about something a little easier. How are you?"

That was *not* easier, but it should have been. "I don't know. I think I'm all right and then *bam* there's his old craggy face just an inch from mine and it's all right there again." Eugene McArthur was my own personal demon; the only question was would he haunt me forever?

"It just happened, Hennessy." She sighed and stopped pushing the stroller and smiled down at Stone sleeping before casting a more serious glance at me.

"You must take all the time you need to get over what happened." Peaches held up a hand to stop the denial perched on the tip of my tongue. "I know your first instinct is to say you're fine, and maybe you genuinely are, but this is hard shit to get over Hennessy. Trust me."

Her eyes were haunted and it was the first hint I'd seen that her life wasn't perfect. "Allow yourself to feel what you feel. Angry that it happened, frustrated, pissed off at the world. Feel them all. Talk to a therapist. Fuck it out. Whatever you gotta do, do it."

"Speaking from experience?"

"Hell, yeah." She pushed the stroller and told me a little bit about her work for the government and the problems that brought her to Texas.

"It was an ongoing problem and the effects have been…lasting."

"So I need to find a way to deal with it or let it destroy me?"

"Pretty much. Hardtail Ranch is a great place to recover, if one was so inclined."

I laughed. "Subtlety is not your strong suit, Peaches. Anyone ever tell you that?"

"Not to my face."

The look of innocence she tried for was so off the mark I couldn't help but laugh. That one act, that laugh, the movement of stretching my mouth into a grin, gave me hope that Peaches was right. That eventually things would get back to something resembling normal.

"Seriously," she asked, "do you plan on sticking around?"

I wanted to, more with each passing day. But it wasn't up to me, not really. "I don't know, I guess it's something we'll have to talk about. I mean, now that there's no reason for us to stay married, maybe Cruz wants his independence back. Or his living space." Though I could think of worse things than being in close quarters with Cruz.

"A little unsolicited advice?"

I nodded because I didn't have any girlfriends, and Peaches was just the kind of straight talker I liked.

"If you want to stay, stay. Don't have a talk with Cruz because it'll scare him, or worse, make him come up with some convoluted rationale for why leaving is best for you. Just tell him that you're staying and that you guys are doing this relationship thing for real."

Peaches spoke with such confidence I almost believed it was that easy.

Almost. "Just like that?"

She nodded and waved a dismissive hand in the air. "These guys are great. They really are true American heroes because they will run towards the gunshots, the fire, the shit show, and they'll do it all to save everyone who lives on this ranch. But going after some really scary shit like love and happily ever after? Well that's where *our* strength as women comes in."

I liked that, the idea that my emotions were a strength instead of the weakness I'd always considered them. "Maybe you're right Peaches."

"I am right," she said confidently and shrugged her shoulders.

Maybe she was right and it was my turn to be bold and brave. To go after exactly what I wanted instead of merely existing. Right now, the only thing I wanted was Cruz. All day. Everyday. Every night. Every fucking minute in between.

He'd already shown me, in so many ways, what kind of man he was. How could I have avoided falling for him? As good as he was, accepting this proposal to help me out, he'd been nothing short of an angel for the past twenty-four hours. A big strong man like him, behaving so gently, had a way of touching a girl down to her soul, and my lonely soul was positively shook.

"You are, right," I agreed.

"Good. Go get him." She nodded into the distance, and I turned in that direction, squinting against the sun to see Cruz's familiar walk headed right towards us.

"I can't." There was something odd about the set of his shoulders, the way he hunched forward against the non-existent chill in the air, like he was protecting himself against something.

"What if he's coming to tell me to pack my things and leave the ranch?"

"He's not. That man has it bad, trust me. I had to keep him in line while you were kidnapped. Sorry," she said when I winced at the word. "He was a fucking mess, pacing and threatening to skin people alive. It was hot. And sweet. And all of that equals him wanting you."

Wanting me in bed maybe, but that would fade. Soon probably.

"Here goes nothing."

"Good luck," Peaches whispered and patted me on the back, punctuating it with a supportive push in his direction.

My legs felt like lead as they ate up the wild grass that surrounded the horse stalls, but my heart soared. With every step I felt lighter and freer, like maybe, just maybe this was one of those pivotal moments in life where taking the chance pays off in a big way. My steps picked up in my eagerness to get to Cruz, to be closer and see the swirling blues of his eyes, the honeyed color of his skin, and the little dimples he tried to hide when he laughed.

My steps slowed as I took in his posture once more. His shoulders were hunched forward, his brows were dipped into a low, angry 'V' and my feet stopped altogether. "What's wrong?"

"It's...fuck, I don't know how to say this to you, Hennessy."

I sucked in a deep breath as my mind played all the possibilities of what Cruz was about to say, landing on the distinct possibility that he was about to kick me out of his life for good.

"Just say it."

I stood still, hands balled into fists at my side with my eyes squeezed tight, as if that would somehow protect me against the words he was about to say.

"Look at me Hennessy."

I shook my head. "I can hear you just fine. Say the words, Cruz."

He sighed and stepped closer. I knew he did because my body was instantly ten degrees hotter.

TIED

"Open your eyes, you stubborn-ass woman."

The amusement in his voice threw me off, and I peeked one eye open.

"What is it? Just tell me. Please."

His arms came around me, tight, holding me close as he whispered in my ear the words I never ever expected to hear.

Injuries too severe. Lost a lot of blood. Internal bleeding. Couldn't save him. It all amounted to one hard fact. Homer was dead. My father was no longer among the living.

"No!" I pushed at his chest but Cruz only held me tighter, determined to be my anchor when the world was threatening to toss me around until I couldn't recover. "No."

"I'm sorry baby. I went to check on him, to see if he needed anything for his stay in the hospital." He spoke in a firm whisper that left no doubt of their truthfulness, especially when combined with the agony in his voice.

"He wanted you to know how sorry he was and how much he loved you. Said you were his greatest accomplishment."

Tears streamed down my face at his softly spoken words, as the image of the Homer I used to know flashed in my mind. Before he was old and gray, before he neglected everything in the name of chasing the next win. Instead, I remembered him when I was a kid, when I was happy for that little bit of pocket change he always gave me and the fistful of candy he always left for me between visits.

Those memories were all I had of Homer now. They would have to be enough.

Chapter Thirty-Two

Cruz

Homer was dead, and I had to be the one to break the news to Hennessy. There were about ten other, better ways I could have broken the news to her other than fucking blurting it out the way I did. But I wasn't known for my eloquence or my tact, so I went with the easiest way to make she sure understood. Her father was dead.

"I'm sorry, Henny baby. So fuckin' sorry."

Her face was blank, expressionless as the words sank in, words she never thought she'd hear, at least not anytime soon.

"No." It was one word, but it was fierce, slicing through my flesh with ease. She stood in front of me, trying like hell not to fall apart. For the first time in my life, I wished I was a man more gifted with words so I could have said it in a way that wouldn't rip her heart out of her chest.

Because now Hennessy's feelings mattered to me. A lot. For real.

When the tears finally broke, I was there. I did what I could and gave her my broad shoulders to fall apart on, and she clung to me. Her fingernails clawed at my shoulders and back as tears poured out of her, along with big, heaving sobs that shook her. Anger and sadness erupted out of her, turning her clawing hands to pounding fists until finally she just leaned into me, pressing her soft weight into me. Confident I'd carry this burden for her, which I was happy to do.

"Hen, babe."

Small aftershocks vibrated her body until finally, minutes later, she ran out of tears. Sort of.

"You know the worst part?" she said.

She shook as if at a memory, and I tried to pretend like this was a perfectly normal conversation.

"How angry Eugene was, and how crazed he looked so filled with vengeance. It flowed from him and there I was, completely fucking powerless to do anything about it."

She shuddered as if suddenly overcome by the memories, days later. "And with every touch, I blamed Homer. I *hated* him. And when Eugene put his mouth on me and his fingers…" she trailed off as the memory shook her. I didn't need to be a genius to figure out the rest of that sentence.

"When he did that, I wished him dead, Cruz. I wished my own fucking father dead."

Sobs escaped from her again, and I held her tighter, now understanding her grief.

"None of this shit is your fault, Hennessy. None of it."

I'd kill that old fuckin' mobster a second time if I could, just to relieve her of this pain.

"Homer's injuries were too bad. The doctors did what they could, but he was old and in bad health."

If anything, he died because it took us too long to decide on a plan of action and execute, but I didn't say that to her.

She shook her head again, trying to wiggle out of my grasp without much success.

"No. I wished him fucking dead and now he's dead. Do you have any idea what this feels like? I'm sorry he's dead, but I'm still mad at him. So. Fucking. Mad."

Her words were muffled by tears and I debated on whether or not to share one final piece of bad news. "What? What else do you have for me?"

My gaze was completely focused on Hen and her red hair, those fiery green eyes that even now, hadn't lost their spark.

"Just say it, Cruz. Whatever it is, just spit it the fuck out. Please."

One frustrated hand swiped away at tears that kept falling, and the other pushed a fat red curl from her face.

I sucked in a deep breath and just blurted it out. Again. "Homer had stage two cancer. It was treatable, but he'd already decided against treatment."

How the fuck it was possible for her skin to get even paler, I wasn't sure, but she turned transparent at the news. "How long?"

"Does it matter?"

"How fucking long? Tell me."

"At least two months according to the records the doctor had." Thankfully, Opey was a small town and knowing everybody had its perks.

Instead of crying or screaming or railing against the world, she shocked the hell out of me when she laughed. Even though tears continued to stream down her cheeks, she kept on laughing until the sound turned from amused to bitter. Brittle. Angry.

"Now it all makes sense. It's fucked up as hell, but it all makes sense. He knew he wouldn't make it out alive and had probably decided to bet it all knowing he was dying." Another brittle laugh escaped. Hen was about to go full blown psycho. "I'm not sure if that makes it better or worse, honestly."

It made me wish I'd been the one to kill that fucker.

"Thanks Cruz, for letting me know."

I wasn't ready to walk away from Hennessy. Hell I wasn't sure I would ever be ready for that, but I knew right now she needed space. She needed time to process her feelings about Homer's death and all the other fucked up shit she'd been through since before she crash landed at Hardtail Ranch.

"I'm here if you need me, Hen."

She turned at my words and smiled. It was sad, almost wistful, but it was a real smile, and there was a hint of something else in her eyes that kept hope alive.

I watched her walk away with purposeful strides that said she was back to trying to keep her emotions in check. She could have her space for now, but soon we would talk.

Then, I would make her mine.

TIED

For real.

Chapter Thirty-Three

Hennessy

Standing there in the middle of the clearing Peaches and Aspen had chosen as a final resting spot for Homer's ashes, I was angry, and I was sad. And wishing the end of this day didn't meant that I'd have to say goodbye to Cruz, as well. Two men who'd both left indelible impressions on my heart, and I had to say goodbye to both of them on the same damn day. Life was a cruel bitch sometimes.

But today wasn't about the unfairness of life. Or me. Or Cruz. It was about Homer, mediocre father, terrible husband, and degenerate gambler. He was all of that and probably a lot more to other people in this world, but he was also gone from this world. No longer, hopefully, capable of causing pain to others. Or to himself. It was a small blessing, but it still hurt.

"Sweetheart, I am so so sorry for your loss."

My mom, Sissy, had arrived yesterday afternoon with my stepfather, Grant. If they were at all surprised to find me here with Cruz, neither of them had said anything. Yet.

"So, so sorry." She wrapped her thin frame around mine and Grant in turn wrapped his big frame, so much like Cruz's, around us both.

"I know, Mom. Thanks." I let her hug me, more because she needed it more than I did. In the week since I found out about his death, I had cried plenty, mostly for myself, but tears don't give a shit. They fall regardless.

"It means a lot that you came." I knew she had loved Homer, and if he'd been capable of getting his shit together, we'd still be one big happy family. But she was happier with Grant than anytime I could remember before he came into our lives, which made me happy for her.

"At least now he's done gambling." Mom sighed in that way of hers that was part nervous tick and part embarrassment over emotions she felt were inappropriate. You'd think she grew up rich with the way she kept up with ridiculous rules of etiquette.

I nodded at her words. "It's fine, Mom. He wasn't a good man, but it's still sad that he's gone. The few good memories I have of him are the only ones I'll ever have now, and that's okay."

"Oh, honey." She wrapped her bony arms around me in another hug and pressed a kiss to my cheek, practically vibrating with anxiety and grief.

"This is an incredible view. Homer would have appreciated it once upon a time."

"He would have. It reminds me of a spot near Black Hawk that he always visited. Whether he won or lost, he'd take me up there and say, Henny this is what life is all about. It was total bullshit of course, but he did seem to really appreciate the view."

"That's nice, honey." That was her default when she didn't know what to say, and I just smiled, happy to end the small talk. All the talk, honestly.

Except Cruz chose that moment to join us and clasped our hands together before he pressed an affectionate kiss to my temple. The panty-melting spot and my panties melted right there at my father's funeral. I didn't miss the wide-eyed stare my mom shared with Grant, but I chose to keep silent on the matter.

"Sissy. Dad. Thanks for coming," Cruz said.

Grant's slightly lighter but still dirty blond brows furrowed into a disapproving scowl. "Just what the hell is going on here? You two look awful cozy." He shook his head and scoffed in disgust. "You're *related* for fuck's sake!"

Cruz scoffed and held me tighter, whether it was for his sake or my own, I wasn't sure, but I leaned into him because it felt damn good.

"You're barely a father so spare me the family shit, *Dad*. Not now and definitely not here."

There had always been tension between them which I'd always chalked up to Cruz's loyalty to Esme, but now it seemed like something more.

"This isn't right, Cruz, you have to see that."

Cruz didn't have to see anything, judging from his expression when he stepped into Grant's face. "We're one big happy fucking family, are we?"

He looked around at the rest of the Reckless Bastards, gathered in smaller circles with their women and children. Without all the leather, denim, and tattoos, it could have been any small town American family event.

"Yeah, we are."

"Then why is it that neither you nor Sissy knew that Homer bet his daughter in a goddamn poker game? That the fuckin' gangster who *won her* tracked her down all the way to Texas? Because Hennessy came here, *to me*, to help her. And you know what I did? I did what family is supposed to do. I married her to keep her safe. What the fuck did you do?"

Grant floundered, his mouth opening and closing like a fish gasping its last breath and Cruz laughed.

"That's what I thought. It's done and we don't need your blessing—or your goddamn permission."

I sank into Cruz's masculine warmth when he pulled me close again and kissed my forehead, thankful he didn't go into any more detail of my ordeal.

Mom sucked in a horrified breath, complete with her hands over her heart just in case it chose this moment to leap from her chest.

"Oh my sweet girl," she said and flung her arms around Cruz. "Thank you so much for keeping her safe."

"You're welcome," he grunted in that gruff tone I'd grown to love since coming here and getting reacquainted with Cruz. He was uncomfortable as hell but Cruz accepted all the love Mom heaped on him because apparently, she needed to do it.

"I'm happy to keep Hennessy safe. She's special to me."

Mom looked at him and then me, a wide beaming smile. "She sure is. It's the luck of the Irish. That's what Homer used to say."

"I remember that. The red hair and green eyes. He said I was even better than a four leaf clover." Not that it had helped him win more than a handful of times.

"I guess you stepped up." Grant reluctantly offered praise as he always did, bitter that Cruz had already surpassed his achievements.

"I always step up." Cruz's words were punctuated by the possessive way he gripped me at the hips. "Always."

Grant nodded, accepting his son's words at face value but not the spirit of them.

"Makes sense. Now that the trouble is over, you'll get an annulment. I'll get you in touch my lawyer."

His expectant tone rubbed me and Cruz the wrong way, but I knew Cruz had this. His chest expanded with one controlled breath and his deep blue gaze looked into matching royal blue eyes with steely determination.

"When Hennessy and I figure it out, we'll let you know. Excuse us."

"Tell me that was as awful as it felt," I whispered to him as soon as we were out of ear shot of our parents.

"It wasn't as bad as I expected, but it wasn't pleasant. Having you there helped." The way he held my face and cupped it gently made me feel cherished. Precious. I smiled up and accepted his sweet kiss that quickly turned smoldering.

"You good?"

I nodded, because I knew what he was asking. I *was* okay and I would be okay. It was time to officially say goodbye to Homer.

"As good as I can be, but yeah, I think I'm on the road to peace and recovery and all that healthy bullshit."

He laughed, and I joined in before grabbing his face and kissing the hell out of him. "I'm pretty sure it's all thanks to you, Cruz."

And I hoped like hell that today wouldn't be the last day I got to spend with him.

"I'm pretty sure it was all you, but I'll take the compliment."

When Cruz wrapped his arms around me and squeezed, I felt really and truly loved. Not for the first time in my life, but this was the first time I felt it from someone other than my mom and grandparents. And it felt really fucking good. As in, *a girl could get used to this* kind of good.

"We'll talk about everything else later. For now, go heal and shit."

He winked and smacked my ass, wearing a big proud smile as I turned towards the front of the gathered crowd.

Time to say goodbye to Homer. "Thanks. And Cruz?"

"Yeah?"

"We *will* talk. Tonight."

A smile spread and it was wide and gorgeous and it stole my breath.

"Bet your sweet ass we will, babe."

Exactly the words I wanted to hear, and I walked forward, through the crowd and toward the podium set up with the Reckless Bastards emblem on it. I stood in front of the rag tag group that was equal part friends and family, took a deep breath and gave Homer a proper send off to the afterlife.

Chapter Thirty-Four

Cruz

"What are we doing here?"

Hennessy was emotionally exhausted, a little raw and not in the mood for anything that went off script. The stiff way she'd been holding herself since she gave Homer's eulogy told of her stress and inner turmoil, and I hated there was nothing I could do to ease it.

I leaned in and flashed a flirtatious smile. "It's called a surprise, Hennessy. Are you familiar with the concept?"

She rolled her eyes, and said, "Smartass."

Still, she put her hand in mine and let me guide her through the upper level and down to the dimly lit lower level. Instead of turning right, we went left to the big private room that was usually closed off.

"Should I be worried?"

"You should be terrified," I told her and ran one fingertip from her collarbone down to her palm. "And turned the fuck on."

"Done. And done." I chuckled at her honesty and unlocked the door, pushing it open and stepping aside so Hen could see all the shit I'd done to make this special for us. Both of us.

"Holy. Shit." She sucked in a breath and the wonder in her eyes hit me straight in the cock. It strengthened my resolve. No matter what else happened tonight, we would talk.

"It's like a sex playground."

"I figured we could both use a little bit of fun with the day, hell the past few weeks, we've had."

I knew I could use it, and if any of the fantasies she shared with me over this past week were close to true, she could too. I wouldn't push her, not ever, but I wanted this. With her. Right now.

"What do you think?"

I held my breath and waited for her response, which felt like it took forever to come.

"I think it sounds like a really good plan. Really good," she said again breathlessly. Her porcelain skin was flushed pink, green eyes were more emerald, with desire than anything else, and her chest rose and fell quicker and quicker.

"The question is, where should we begin?" There was a playful tone in her voice that hadn't been there earlier that made me smile.

If Hennessy wanted to play, I was more than happy to indulge. "You choose."

She scanned the room, tapping her chin in thought as her gaze landed on one contraption after another. I knew, a breath before she chose, which one had piqued her interest.

"How about that swing? It looks like it could be…interesting."

Before my gaze even landed on the black leather swing made up of leather and nylon straps, an image appeared in my mind of her butt naked, nothing but her flaming red hair visible among the darkness and leather.

"I'm definitely interested."

She tossed her head back and laughed, moving toward the swing where she quickly undressed.

"Good to know. I've never used one of these before, have you?"

I shook my head, but Hennessy was too distracted by figuring out the swing, which gave me the perfect opportunity to help. Sort of.

"Good?"

She looked up at me through auburn lashes and blinked, skin flushed and slightly out of breath. "Good isn't the word I'd use, but yeah."

"Good." Now that I had her right where I wanted her, it was time to talk. "I was skeptical about you when you first showed up here."

"No kidding," she snorted and shook her head. "You weren't as diplomatic as you'd like to think about that particular fact."

I smiled. "I was kind of a dick, right?"

She nodded. "A bit, but I understood. It was a big ask."

"A big fucking ask," I clarified, letting my fingertips skate up and down the inside of her spread thighs. "It didn't matter that you were hot as fuck and clearly trouble on two legs. I didn't want to say yes to you, but I couldn't say no."

Hen blinked, finally realizing this wasn't foreplay. Not yet, anyway. "You could have. You probably should have, even though I'm glad as hell you didn't."

"Me, too." I could barely focus with her spread wide before me, pussy pink and glistening, swollen with desire. I couldn't resist slipping one finger inside, and the moan she rewarded me with sent a poker of heat straight to my cock.

"I couldn't have walked away from you Hennessy; I just didn't realize it at the time."

It had taken a long damn time for me to understand how I felt about her and what the fuck it all meant, but now that I knew, there was no going back.

She looked up at me with big green eyes, sparkling like gems with fear and hope and uncertainty. "Now that you know, what do you plan to do about it?"

Good fucking question. "I plan to keep you here with me for as long as I can. Not just in my bed for sex and not just here for kinky fun shit like this, Hen. I want it all. You. Your big heart and your sexy ass body."

She sucked in a shocked breath, and I let the pride fill my chest and kept going. "I want to have a few kids with you running around this ranch, or maybe a plot of land of our own. I want to see your belly grow with our babies, and I want to see that red fade to silver as smile lines take over your face. I want to know what it feels like to love you at forty-five. Fifty-five. Eighty. Hell, forever."

She shuddered at my touch, or maybe it was my words. Her head fell back and her legs went slack as my finger pumped in and out of her. "Cruz."

"I'm right here, Hen. Waiting for an answer." But while I waited, I was more than happy to explore the heat of her wet pussy. She panted and let out soft whimpers while I made her feel good, unable to look away from her face twisted in passion.

Instead of answering, she grabbed my wrists and ground against my hand in search of her pleasure. Her gaze never left mine and her grip never loosened as she humped and ground her way to a violent orgasm that nearly ripped her in half.

"Cruz! Oh, fuck! Fuck! Fuck! Fuck!"

I laughed. "Acceptable."

She grinned. "Smart ass."

Her body relaxed completely and my fingers slipped from her body, slick and shining under the dim lights of the room. The scent wafted to my nostrils, and

I couldn't resist a taste of what was to come, sliding the finger in my mouth and sucking it with a groan.

"Oh shit," she moaned and tossed her head back.

"I'm still waiting on that answer, Hennessy."

"Answer," she frowned. "Answer to what?"

"Hennessy," I growled.

She laughed. "Sorry. I'm being naughty. Maybe you should punish me until I give you the answer you want to hear?"

"Maybe I should." It was exactly the right answer, and I grabbed her ankle ties and fixed them to the swing legs, leaving her pussy spread wide and exposed to me. "Remember the question?"

Her lips curved into a playful smile, and I licked her asshole, loving the way she nearly jumped out of the chair, except the restraints made it impossible for her to move, and she just moaned. Again.

"Maybe?"

Yep, I loved playful Hennessy, and it was time she knew it.

"I love you, Hennessy, and I want you here with me. Forever. For everything."

I licked her pussy long and slow, taking my time until a long, moaning cry fell from her lips.

"Marriage," I whispered and slipped my tongue inside her wet pussy. "Babies." I kissed her clit. "Growing old together. All of it." My hands massaged her inner thighs while I licked and sucked at her, making her vibrate and shake with pleasure.

"Cruz, please." She squirmed and bucked in an effort get closer or put some distance between us, I didn't know which, but I fucking loved it. She was at my mercy, only able to accept the pleasure I heaped on her with my mouth and my tongue. My fingers. And eventually, my cock.

"Yes, Cruz! Please! More!"

It was too much. It felt too fucking good. *She* felt too fucking good, hot and wet and tight, the perfect pussy trifecta. I shed my clothes and stroked my cock as Hen reached for me and tried to wrap her hand around it.

"Hennessy," I growled when she moaned in frustration that the bindings were too restrictive.

She looked up at me from her upside down position with a smile as she stroked my cock and my balls with her tongue, teasing me.

"Nice and hard," she moaned and reached her head forward, wrapping her lips around my cock.

My hips bucked and Hennessy opened up, taking me as deep as she could, with a smile even though she was completely at my mercy. The trust it indicated was humbling, and my dick went even harder just thinking about what it meant.

"Oh fuck, Hen!" She took me deep, sliding her tongue along the underside of my sack and sucked me like her life depended on it.

TIED

My hips bucked and pumped into her, fucked her plump mouth like it was as sweet and tight as her cunt. "Hennessy!"

She sucked me hard, ignoring my words and not even phased when my cock slipped too far down her throat. She only moaned and cried, giving me everything she could.

It wasn't enough. I needed to bury myself inside all the creamy wetness between her thighs. I spun her around and slid deep in one long stroke. "Fuck me, Hen."

"That's my line," she said on a long groan as her eyes rolled in the back of her head. Her nipples were as hard as pink rocks, puckered and straining towards my mouth. Her skin was flushed from desire and unspent need. "Cruz. Please."

I gripped her hips and pounded into her, hard and fast because the position was always perfect. Hen was exactly where I needed her to be, and I fucked her like hers was the first pussy that ever mattered, because it was. I fucked her like it was so much more than fucking, because that's exactly what it was, an out of body erotic experience that compared to nothing else.

"Hennessy, oh fuck!"

"Yes!" I pinched her hard nipples because I couldn't *not* do it and her pussy clamped tight around me, and a long low growl escaped slowly. The harder I squeezed, the more she bucked against me and the more she pulled my cock into her body. "Yes, Cruz! Fuck me, oh yes!"

I smiled and gave one final pinch before we both flew apart together, into a million brilliant pieces, before we collapsed back to earth.

Together.

Time stood still in those moments where we were both breathless and panting, smiling at each other like fools.

"That was…holy shit, Cruz."

I laughed as masculine pride swelled in my chest. "It was, wasn't it?"

She nodded. "Did you mean what you said?" Her question was serious, almost pleading.

"Every fucking word."

Her shoulders sank in relief, like those were the three words she was waiting to hear, instead of the ones I said earlier.

"Awesome, because I think it sounds like one hell of a future you're promising Cruz. The love. The marriage. The babies. All of it."

"And it's one I plan to deliver on. You in?"

"You bet your sweet ass I'm in, babe, because I love you too."

I thought I'd experienced all the good highs in life, finishing basic training for the Army and then Special Forces. Leaving the Army. Becoming a Reckless Bastard. But then a fiery redhead I'd never expected to see again landed on my doorstep and changed everything.

"That's really good to hear. Real damn good, Hen."

She laughed and wriggled in the swing, before remembering she was still bound and tied, and at my mercy. "Yeah?"

"Hell yeah," I told her.

Her challenge was short and sweet. "Show me."

I showed her with every drop of love and energy within my body. I loved on her on the swing, I tapped the leather crop to her smooth creamy ass and used half a dozen toys to make her come as many times as she could.

It was the first night of the rest of our lives, and I wanted to make damn sure we both remembered it.

For the rest of our lives together.

And beyond.

THE END

Acknowledgements

Thank you so much for making my books a success! I appreciate all of you! Thanks to all of my beta readers, street teamers, ARC readers and Facebook fans. Y'all are THE BEST!

And a huge very special thanks to Jessie! I'm such a *hot mess, but without your keen sense of organization and skills, I'd be a burny fiery inferno of hot mess!! Thank you!

And a very special thanks to my editors (who sometimes have to work all through the night! *See HOT MESS above!) Thank you for making my words make sense.

Copyright © 2020 KB Winters and BookBoyfriends Publishing Inc

KB WINTERS

About The Author

KB Winters is a Wall Street Journal and USA Today Bestselling Author of steamy hot books about Bikers, Billionaires, Bad Boys and Badass Military Men. Just the way you like them. She has an addiction to caffeine, tattoos and hard-bodied alpha males. The men in her books are very sexy, protective and sometimes bossy, her ladies are...well...*bossier*!

Living in sunny Southern California, with her amazing man and fur babies, this embarrassingly hopeless romantic writes every chance she gets!

You can reach KB at Facebook.com/kbwintersauthor and at kbwintersauthor@gmail.com

Copyright © 2020 KB Winters and BookBoyfriends Publishing Inc

Printed in Great Britain
by Amazon